Asimov's Choice:
Comets & Computers

Asimov's Choice: Comets & Computers

George Scithers, General Editor of the Isaac Asimov Science Fiction Magazine

Distributed in Canada, U.K. and Australia by Magnum Books
ISBN 0-458-93550-6

Library of Congress Catalog Number: 78-51864
ISBN 0-89559-022-0
Printed in the United States of America

Grateful acknowledgment is hereby made for permission to reprint the following:
Grimes at Glenrowan by A. Bertram Chandler; © 1978 by Davis Publications, Inc.; reprinted by permission of Scott Meredith Literary Agency, Inc.
The Third Dr. Moreau by Martin Gardner; © 1978 by Davis Publications, Inc.; reprinted by permission of the author.
The Small Stones of Tu Fu by Brian W. Aldiss; © 1978 by Davis Publications, Inc.; reprinted by permission of Southmoor Serendipity, Ltd.
A Hideous Splotch of Purple by Theresa Harned; © 1978 by Davis Publications, Inc.; reprinted by permission of the author.
Will Academe Kill Science Fiction? by Jack Williamson; © 1978 by Davis Publications, Inc.; reprinted by permission of Scott Meredith Literary Agency, Inc.
Heal the Sick, Raise the Dead by Jesse Peel; © 1978 by Davis Publications, Inc.; reprinted by permission of the author.
Roboroots by Jay A. Parry; © 1978 by Davis Publications, Inc.; reprinted by permission of the author.
Chariot Ruts by Pamela F. Service; © 1978 by Davis Publications, Inc.; reprinted by permission of the author.
Lost and Found by Michael A. Banks and George Wagner; © 1978 by Davis Publications, Inc.; reprinted by permission of the authors.
Darkside by Gary D. McClellan; © 1978 by Davis Publications, Inc.; reprinted by permission of the author.
The Agony of Defeat by Jack C. Haldeman II; © 1978 by Davis Publications, Inc.; reprinted by permission of the author.
The Far King by Richard Wilson; © 1978 by Davis Publications, Inc.; reprinted by permission of the author.

CONTENTS

Cover Painting by Greg Theakston. Interior drawings by Frank Kelly Freas, Rick Sternbach, George Barr, Alex Schomburg, Freff, Dan Simpson, Vincent D. Fate, & Jack Gaughan

EDITORIAL: EXTRAORDINARY VOYAGES

One of the pet parlor games played by those interested in science fiction—writers, editors, fans, readers—is to define science fiction. What the devil is it? How do you differentiate it from fantasy? From general fiction?

There are probably as many definitions as there are definers; and the definitions range from those of the extreme exclusionists, who want their science fiction pure and hard, to those of the extreme inclusionists who want their science fiction to embrace everything in sight.

Here is an extreme exclusionist definition of my own: "Science fiction deals with scientists working at science in the future."

Here is an extreme inclusionist definition of John Campbell's: "Science fiction stories are whatever science fiction editors buy."

A moderate definition (again mine) is: "Science fiction is that branch of literature that deals with human responses to changes in the level of science and technology." This leaves it open as to whether the changes are advances or retrogressions, and whether, with the accent on "human response" one need do more than refer glancingly and without detail to those changes.

To some writers, in fact, the necessity for discussing science seems so minimal that they object to the use of the word in the name of the genre. They prefer to call whatever it is they write "speculative fiction," thus keeping the abbreviation "S F."*

Ocassionally, I feel the need to think it all out afresh and so why not approach the definition historically. For instance—

What is the first product of western literature, which we have intact, and which could be considered by inclusionists to be science fiction?

How about Homer's *Odyssey*? It doesn't deal with science in a world which had not yet invented it; but it does deal with the equivalent of extra-terrestrial monsters, like Polyphemus, and with people disposing of the equivalent of an advanced science, like Circe.

Yet most people would think of the *Odyssey* as a "travel tale."

But that's all right. The two views are not necessarily mutually exclusive. The "travel tale," after all, was the original fantasy, the natural fantasy. Why not? Until contemporary times, travel was the arduous luxury of the very few, who alone could see that which the vast hordes of humanity could not.

Most people, till lately, lived and died in the same town, the same valley, the same patch of earth, in which they were born. To them, whatever lay beyond the horizon was fantasy. It could be anything—and anything told of that distant wonderland fifty miles away could be believed. Pliny was not too sophisticated to believe the fantasies he was told of distant lands, and a thousand years of readers believed Pliny. Sir John Mandeville had no trouble passing off his fictional travel tales as the real thing.

And for twenty-five centuries after Homer, when anyone wanted to write a fantasy, he wrote a travel tale.

Imagine someone who goes to sea, lands upon an unknown island, and finds wonders. Isn't that Sinbad the Sailor and his tales of the Rukh and of the Old Man of the Sea? Isn't that Lemuel Gulliver and his encounters with Lilliputians and Brobdingnagians? As a matter of fact, isn't that King Kong?

*I don't favor the term "speculative fiction" except insofar as it might abolish that abominable abbreviation "sci-fi." But then it might substitute "spec-fic" which is even worse.

The Lord of the Rings, together with what promises to be a vast horde of slavish imiations, is a travel tales, too.

Yet are not these travel tales fantasies, rather than science fiction? Where does "real" science fiction come in?

Consider the first professional science fiction writer; the first writer who made his living out of undoubted science fiction—Jules Verne. He didn't think of himself as writing science fiction, for the term had not yet been invented, and for a dozen years he wrote for the French stage with indifferent success.

But he was a frustrated traveller and explorer and in 1863, he suddenly hit pay-dirt with his book *Five Weeks in a Balloon.* He thought of the book as a travel tale, but an unusual one since it made use of a device made possible by scientific advance.

Verne followed up his success by using other scientific devices, of the present and possible future, to carry his heroes farther and farther afield in other "voyages extraordinaire"—to the polar regions, to the sea-bottom, to the Earth's center, to the Moon.

The Moon had been a staple of the tellers of travel tales ever since Lucian of Samosata in the 1st Century A.D. It was thought of as just another distant land, but what made it different in Verne's case was that he made the effort to get his heroes there by scientific principles that had not yet been applied in real life (though his method was unworkable as described).

After him, other writers took men on longer voyages to Mars and to other planets; and finally, in 1928, E. E. Smith, in his *The Skylark of Space,* broke all bonds with his "inertialess drive" and carried humanity out to the distant stars.

So science fiction began as an outgrowth of the travel tale, differing chiefly in that the conveyances used did not yet exist but might exist if the level of science and technology were extrapolated to greater heights in the future.

But surely not all science fiction can be viewed as travel tales. What of stories that remain right here on Earth but deal with robots, or with nuclear or ecological disaster, or with new interpretations of the distant past for that matter?

None of that, however, is "right here" on Earth. Following Verne's lead, whatever happens on Earth is made possible by continuing changes (usually advances) in the level of science and technology so that the story must take place "right there" on future Earth.

What, then, do you think of this definition: "Science fiction stories are extraordinary voyages into any of the infinite supply of conceivable futures."?

—Of which we have samples right here in this issue, and in every issue.

—Isaac Asimov

GRIMES AT GLENROWAN
by A. Bertram Chandler

Captain Chandler reports that he wrote his first story after meeting John W. Campbell, the late, great editor of Astounding/Analog SF, *during WW II. During the war years, the author became a regular contributor to the SF magazines, but almost dropped out of the field when he was promoted to Chief Officer in the British-Australian steamship service. His wife, Susan, encouraged him to take up writing again; the Rim Worlds and the Rim Runners series is a result.*

Sternbach

Commodore John Grimes of the Rim Worlds Naval Reserve, currently Master of the survey ship *Faraway Quest,* was relaxing in his day cabin aboard that elderly but trustworthy vessel. That morning, local time, he had brought the old ship down to a landing at Port Fortinbras, on Elsinore, the one habitable planet in orbit about the Hamlet sun. It was Grimes's first visit to Elsinore for very many years. This call was to be no more—and no less—than a showing of the flag of the Confederacy. The *Quest* had been carrying out a survey of a newly discovered planetary system rather closer to the Shakespearean Sector than to the Rim Worlds and Grimes's lords and masters back on Lorn had instructed him, on completion of this task, to pay a friendly call on their opposite numbers on Elsinore.

However, he would be seeing nobody of any real importance until this evening, when he would attend a reception being held in his honor at the President's palace. So he had time to relax, at ease in his shipboard shorts and shirt, puffing contentedly at his vile pipe, watching the local trivia programs on his playmaster. That way he would catch up on the planetary news, learn something of Elsinorian attitudes and prejudices. He was, after all, visiting this world in an ambassadorial capacity.

He looked with wry amusement into the screen. There he was—or, to be more exact, there was *Faraway Quest*—coming down. *Not bad,* he admitted smugly, *not bad at all.* There had been a nasty, gusty wind at ground level about which Aerospace Control had failed to warn him—but he had coped. He watched the plump, dull-silver spindle that was his ship sagging to leeward, leaning into the veering breeze, then settling almost exactly into the center of the triangle of bright flashing marker beacons, midway between the Shakespearean Line's *Oberon* and the Commission's *Epsilon Orionis.* He recalled having made a rather feeble joke about O'Brian and O'Ryan. (His officers had laughed dutifully.) He watched the beetle-like ground cars carrying the port officials scurry out across the grey apron as the *Quest*'s ramp was extruded from her after airlock. He chuckled softly at the sight of Timmins, his Chief Officer, resplendent in his best uniform, standing at the head of the gangway to receive the boarding party. Although only a reservist—like Grimes himself—that young man put on the airs and graces of a First Lieutenant of a Constellation Class battlewagon, a flagship at that. But he was a good spaceman and that was all that really mattered.

After a short interval, filled with the chatter of the commentator, he was privileged to watch himself being interviewed by the newsman who had accompanied the officials on board. Did he really look as crusty as that? He wondered. And wasn't there something in what Sonya, his wife, was always saying—and what other ladies had said long before he first met her—about his ears? Stun's'l ears, jughandle ears. Only a very minor operation would be required to make them less outstanding, but . . . He permitted himself another chuckle. He liked him the way that he was and if the ladies didn't they had yet to show it.

The intercom telephone buzzed. Grimes turned to look at Timmins' face in the little screen. He made a downward gesture of his hand towards the playmaster, and his own voice and that of the interviewer at once faded into inaudibility. "Yes, Mr. Timmins?" he asked.

"Sir, there is a lady here to see you."

A lady? wondered Grimes. Elsinore was one of the few worlds upon which he had failed to enjoy a temporary romance. He had been there only once before, when he was a junior officer in the Federation's Survey Service. He recalled (it still rankled) that he had had his shore leave stopped for some minor misdemeanor.

"A lady?" he repeated. Then, "What does she want?"

"She says that she is from Station Yorick, sir. She would like to interview you."

"But I've already been interviewed," said Grimes.

"Not by Station Yorick," a female voice told him. "Elsinore's purveyors of entertainment and philosophy."

Trimmins' face in the little screen had been replaced by that of a girl—a woman, rather. Glossy black hair, short cut, over a thin, creamily pale face with strong bone structure and delicately cleft chin . . . a wide, scarlet mouth . . . almost indigo blue eyes set off by black lashes.

"Mphm," grunted Grimes approvingly. "Mphm. . ."

"Commodore Grimes?" she asked in a musical contralto. "*The* Commodore Grimes?"

"There's only one of me as far as I know," he told her. "And you?"

She smiled whitely. "Kitty, of Kitty's Korner. With a 'K'. And I'd like a *real* interview for *my* audience, not the sort of boring question-and-answer session that you've just been watching."

"Mphm," grunted Grimes again. What harm could it do?, he asked himself. This would be quite a good way of passing what otherwise would be a dull afternoon. And Elsinore was in the Shakespearean Sector, wasn't it? Might not he, Grimes, play Othello to this newshen's Desdemona, wooing her with his tall tales of peril and adventure all over the Galaxy? And in his private grog locker were still six bottles of Antarean Crystal Gold laid aside for emergencies such as this, a potent liquor coarsely referred to by spacemen as a leg-opener, certainly a better loosener of inhibitions than the generality of alcoholic beverages. He would have to partake of it with her, of course, but a couple or three soberups would put him right for the cocktail party.

"Ask Mr. Timmins to show you up," he said.

§ § §

He looked at her over the rim of his glass. He liked what he saw. The small screen of the intercom, showing only her face, had not done her full justice. She sat facing him in an easy chair, making a fine display of slender, well-formed thigh under the high-riding apology for a skirt. (Hemlines were down again, almost to ankle length, in the Rim Worlds and Grimes had not approved of the change in fashion.) The upper part of her green dress was not quite transparent but it was obvious that she neither wore nor needed a bust support.

She looked at him over the rim of her glass. She smiled.

He said, "Here's to Yorick, the Jester. . . ."

She said, "And the philosopher. We have our serious side."

They sipped. The wine was cold, mellow fire.

He said, "Don't we all?"

"You especially," she told him. "You must be more of a philosopher than most men, Commodore. Your interdimensional experiences—"

"So you've heard of them . . . Kitty."

"Yes. Even here. Didn't somebody once say, 'If there's a crack in the Continuum Grimes is sure to fall into it—and come up with the Shaara Crown Jewels clutched in his hot little hands'?"

He laughed. "I've never laid my paws on the Shaara Crown Jewels yet—although I've had my troubles with the Shaara. There was the time that I was in business as an interstellar courier and got tangled with a Rogue Queen—"

But she was not interested in the Shaara. She pressed on, "It seems that it's only out on the Rim proper, on worlds like Kinsolving, that you find these . . . cracks in the Continuum. . . ."

Grimes refilled the glasses saying, "Thirsty work, talking . . ."

"But we've talked hardly at all," she said. "And I *want* you to talk. I want *you* to talk. If all I wanted was stories of high adventure and low adventure in *this* universe I'd only have to interview any of our own space captains. What I want, what Station

Yorick wants, what our public wants is a story such as only *you* can tell. One of your adventures on Kinsolving . . ."

He laughed. "It's not only on Kinsolving's Planet that you can fall through a crack in the Continuum." He was conscious of the desire to impress her. "In fact, the first time that it happened was on Earth. . . ."

She was suitably incredulous.

"On Earth?" she demanded.

"Too right," he said.

§ § §

I'm a Rim Worlder now [he told her] but I wasn't born out on the Rim. As far as the accident of birth is concerned I'm Terran. I started my spacefaring career in the Interstellar Federation's Survey Service. My long leaves I always spent on Earth, where my parents lived.

Anyhow, just to visualize me as I was then: a Survey Service JG Lieutenant with money in his pocket, time on his hands and, if you must know, between girlfriends. I'd been expecting that— What was her name? Oh, yes. Vanessa. I'd been expecting that she'd be still waiting for me when I got back from my tour of duty. She wasn't. She'd married—of all people!—a sewage conversion engineer.

Anyhow, I spent the obligatory couple of weeks with my parents in The Alice. (The Alice? Oh, that's what Australians call Alice Springs, a city in the very middle of the island continent.) My father was an author. He specialized in historical romances. He was always saying that the baddies of history are much more interesting than the goodies—and that the good baddies and the bad goodies are the most fascinating of all. You've a fine example of that in this planetary system of yours. The names, I mean. The Hamlet sun and all that. Hamlet was rather a devious bastard, wasn't he? And although he wasn't an out and out baddie he could hardly be classed as a goodie.

Well, the Old Man was working on yet another historical novel, this one to be set in Australia. All about the life and hard times of Ned Kelly. You've probably never heard of him—very few people outside Australia have—but he was a notorious bushranger. Bushrangers were sort of highway robbers. Just as the English have Dick Turpin and the Americans have Jesse James, so we have the Kelly gang. (Australia had rather a late start as a nation so has always made the most of its relatively short history.)

According to my respected father this Ned Kelly was more, much more, than a mere bushranger. He was a freedom fighter, striking valiant blows on behalf of the oppressed masses, a sort of Robin Hood. And, like that probably-mythical Robin Hood, he was something of a military genius. Until the end he outwitted the troopers—as the police were called in his day—with ease. He was a superb horseman. He was an innovator. His suit of homemade armor—breast- and back-plates and an odd cylindrical helmet—was famous. It was proof against rifle and pistol fire. He was very big and strong and could carry the weight of it.

It was at a place called Glenrowan that he finally came unstuck. In his day it was only a village, a hamlet. (No pun intended.) It was on the railway line from Melbourne to points north. Anyhow, Ned had committed some crime or other at a place called Wangaratta and a party of police was on the way there from Melbourne by special train, not knowing that the Kelly gang had ridden back to Glenrowan. Like all guerrilla leaders throughout history Kelly had an excellent intelligence service. He knew that the train was on the way and would be passing through Glenrowan. He persuaded a gang of Irish workmen—platelayers, they were called—to tear up the railway tracks just north of the village. The idea was that the train would be derailed and the policemen massacred. While the bushrangers were waiting they enjoyed quite a party in the Glenrowan Hotel; Kelly and his gang were more popular than otherwise among the locals. But the schoolmaster—who was *not* a Kelly supporter—managed to creep away from the festivities and, with a lantern and his wife's red scarf, flagged the train down.

The hotel was besieged. It was set on fire. The only man who was not killed at once was Kelly himself. He came out of the smoke and the flames, wearing his armor, a revolver (a primitive multi-shot projectile pistol) in each hand, blazing away at his enemies. One of the troopers had the intelligence to fire at his legs, which were not protected by the armour, and brought him down.

He was later hanged.

§ § §

Well, as I've indicated, my Old Man was up to the eyebrows in his research into the Ned Kelly legend, and some of his enthusiasm rubbed off on to me. I thought that I'd like to have a look at this Glenrowan place. Father was quite amused. He told me that Glenrowan *now* was nothing at all like Glenrowan *then*, that instead of a tiny huddle of shacks by the railway line I should find a not-so-small city sitting snugly in the middle of all-the-year-round-producing orchards under the usual featureless plastic domes. There was, he conceded, a sort of reconstruction of the famous hotel standing beside a railway line—all right for tourists, he sneered, but definitely not for historians.

I suppose that he was a historian—he certainly always took his researches seriously enough—but I wasn't. I was just a spaceman with time on my hands. And—which probably decided me—there was a quite fantastic shortage of unattached popsies in The Alice and my luck might be better elsewhere.

So I took one of the tourist airships from Alice Springs to Melbourne and then a really antique railway train—steam-driven yet, although the coal in the tender was only for show; it was a minireactor that boiled the water—from Melbourne to Glenrowan. This primitive means of locomotion, of course, was for the benefit of tourists.

When I dismounted from that horribly uncomfortable coach at Glenrowan Station I ran straight into an old shipmate. Oddly enough—although, as it turned out later, it wasn't so odd—his name was Kelly. He'd been one of the junior interstellar drive engineer officers in the old *Aries*. I'd never liked him much—or him me—but when you're surrounded by planetlubbers you greet a fellow spaceman as though he were a long-lost brother.

"Grimes!" he shouted. "Gutsy Grimes in person!"

[No, Kitty, I didn't get that nickname because I'm exceptionally brave. It was just that some people thought I had an abnormally hearty appetite and would eat *anything*.]

"An' what are *you* doin' here?" he demanded. His Irish accent, as Irish accents usually do, sounded phony as all hell.

I told him that I was on leave and asked him if he was too. He told me that he'd resigned his commission some time ago and that so had his cousin, Spooky Byrne. Byrne hadn't been with us in *Aries* but I had met him. He was a PCO—Psionic Communications Officer. A Commissioned Teacup Reader, as we used to call them. A trained and qualified telepath. You don't find many of 'em these days in the various merchant services—the Carlotti Communications System is a far more reliable way of handling instantaneous communications over the light-years. But most navies still employ them—a telepath is good for much more than the mere transmission and reception of signals.

So, Kelly and Spooky Byrne, both in Glenrowan. And me, also in Glenrowan. There are some locations in some cities where, it is said, if you loaf around long enough you're sure to meet everybody you know. An exaggeration, of course, but there *are* focal points. But I wouldn't put the Glenrowan Hotel—that artificially tumbledown wooden shack with its bark roof—synthetic bark, of course—in that category. It looked very small and sordid among the tall, shining buildings of the modern city. Small and sordid? Yes, but—somehow—even though it was an obvious, trashy tourist trap it possessed a certain character. Something of the atmosphere of the original building seemed to have clung to the site.

Kelly said, using one of my own favorite expressions, "Come on in, Grimes. The sun's over the yard-arm."

I must have looked a bit dubious. My one-time shipmate had been quite notorious for never paying for a drink when he could get somebody else to do it. He read my expression. He laughed. "Don't worry, Gutsy. I'm a rich man now—which is more than I was when I was having to make do on my beggarly stipend in the Survey Service—may God rot their cotton socks! Come on in!"

Well, we went into the pub. The inside came up to—or down to—my worst expectations. There was a long bar of rough wood with thirsty tourists lined up along it. There was a sagging calico ceiling. There was a wide variety of antique ironmongery hanging on the walls—kitchen implements, firearms, rusty cutlasses. There were simulated flames flickering in the glass chimneys of battered but well-polished brass oil lamps. The wenches behind the bar were dressed in sort of Victorian costumes—long, black skirts, high-collared, frilly white blouses—although I don't think that in good Queen Victoria's day those blouses would have been as near as dammit transparent and worn over no underwear.

We had rum—not the light, dry spirit that most people are used to these days but sweet, treacly, almost-knife-and-fork stuff. Kelly paid, peeling off credits from a roll that could almost have been used as a bolster. We had more rum. Kelly tried to pay again but I wouldn't let him—although I hoped this party wouldn't last all day. Those prices, in that clipjoint, were making a nasty dent in my holiday money. Then Spooky Byrne drifted in, as colourless and weedy as ever, looking like a streak of ectoplasm frayed at the edges.

He stared at me as though he were seeing a ghost. "Grimes, of all people!" he whispered intensely. "Here, of all places!"

[I sensed, somehow, that his surprise was not genuine.]

"An' why not?" demanded his burly, deceptively jovial cousin. "Spacemen are only tourists in uniform. An' as Grimes is in civvies that makes him even more a tourist."

"The . . . coincidence . . ." hissed Spooky. Whatever his act was he was persisting with it.

"Coincidences are always happenin'," said Kelly, playing up to him.

"Yes, Eddie, but—"

"But what?" I demanded, since it seemed expected of me.

"Mr. Grimes," Spooky told me, "would it surprise you if I told you that one of your ancestors was *here*? Was here *then*?"

"Too right it would," I said. "Going back to the old style Twentieth Century, and the Nineteenth, and further back still, most of my male forebears were seamen." The rum was making me boastfully talkative. "I have a pirate in my family tree. And an Admiral of the Royal Navy, on my mother's side. Her family name is Hornblower. So, Spooky, what the hell would either a Grimes or a Hornblower have been doing here, miles inland, in this nest of highway robbers?" Both Kelly and Byrne gave me dirty looks. "All right, then. Not highway robbers. Bushrangers, if it makes you feel any happier."

And not bushrangers either!" growled Kelly. "Freedom fighters!"

"Hah!" I snorted.

"Freedom fighters!" stated Kelly belligerently. "All right, so they did rob a bank or two. An' so what? In that period rebel organizations often robbed the capitalists to get funds to buy arms and all the rest of it. It was no more than S.O.P."

"Mph," I grunted.

"In any case," said Kelly, "your ancestor was so here. We *know*. Come home with us an' we'll convince you."

So I let those two bastards talk me into accompanying them to their apartment, which was a penthouse atop the Glenrowan Tower. This wasn't by any means the tallest building in the city, although it had been, I learned, when it was built. I remarked somewhat enviously that this was a palatial pad for a spaceman and Kelly told me that he wasn't a spaceman but a businessman and that he'd succeeded, by either clever or lucky investments, in converting a winning ticket in the New Irish Sweep into a substantial fortune. Byrne told him that he should give some credit where credit was due. Kelly told Byrne that graduates of the Rhine Institute are bound, by oath, not to use their psionic gifts for personal enrichment. Byrne shut up.

The living quarters of the penthouse were furnished in period fashion—the Victorian period. Gilt and red plush—dark, carved, varnished wood—heavily framed, sepia-tinted photographs—no, not holograms, but those old *flat* photographs—of heavily bearded worthies hanging on the crimson-and-gold papered walls. One of them I recognized from the research material my father had been using. It was Ned Kelly.

"Fascinating," I said.

"This atmosphere is necessary to our researches," said Byrne. Then, "But come through to the laboratory."

I don't know what I was expecting to see in the other room into which they led me. Certainly not what first caught my attention. What caught my attention? What *demanded* my attention. It was, at first glance, a Mannschenn Drive unit—not a full sized one such as would be found in even a small ship but certainly a bigger one than the mini-Mannschenns you find in lifeboats.

[You've never seen a Mannschenn Drive unit? I must show you ours before you go ashore. And you don't understand how they work? Neither do I, frankly. But it boils down, essentially, to gyroscopes processing in time, setting up a temporal precession field, so that our ships aren't really breaking the light barrier but going astern in time while they're going ahead in space.]

"A Mannschenn Drive unit," I said unnecessarily.

"I built it," said Kelly, not without pride.

"What for?" I asked. "Time Travel?" I sneered.

"Yes," he said.

I laughed. "But it's known to be impossible. A negative field would require the energy of the entire galaxy—"

"Not physical Time Travel," said Spooky Byrne smugly. "Psionic Time Travel, back along the world line stemming from an ancestor. Eddie's ancestor was at Glenrowan. So was mine. So was yours."

"Ned Kelly wasn't married," I said triumphantly.

"And so you have to be married to father a child?" asked Byrnes sardonically. "Come off it, Grimes! *You* should know better than that."

[I did, as a matter of fact. This was after that odd business I'd gotten involved in on El Dorado.]

"All right," I said. "Your ancestor might have been present at the Siege of Glenrowan. Mine was not. At or about that time he was, according to my father—and he's the family historian—second mate of a tramp windjammer. He got himself paid off in Melbourne and, not so long afterwards, was master of a little brig running between Australia and New Zealand. He did leave an autobiography, you know."

"Autobiographies are often self-censored," said Byrne. "That long-ago Captain Grimes, that smugly respectable shipmaster, a pillar, no doubt, of Church and State, had episodes in his past that he would prefer to forget. He did not pay off from his ship in Melbourne in the normal way. He—what was the expression?—jumped ship. He'd had words with his captain, who was a notorious bully. He'd exchanged blows. So he deserted and thought that he'd be safer miles inland. The only work that he could find was with the Irish laborers on the railway."

"How do you know all this?" I asked. "*If* it's true—"

"He told me," said Byrne. "Or he told my ancestor—but I was inside his mind at the time. . . ."

"Let's send him back," said Kelly. "That'll convince him."

"Not . . . yet," whispered Byrne. "Let's show him first what will happen if the special train is, after all, derailed. Let's convince him that it's to his interests to play along with us. The . . . alternative, since Grimes showed up here, is much . . . firmer. But we shall need—*did* need?—that British seaman Grimes, just as George Washington needed his British seaman John Paul Jones. . . ."

"Are you trying to tell me," I asked, "that the squalid squabble at Glenrowan was a crucial point in history?"

"Yes," said Kelly.

I realized that I'd been maneuvered to one of the three chairs facing the Mannschenn Drive unit, that I'd been eased quite gently on to the seat. The chair was made of tubular metal, with a high back, at the top of which was a helmet of metal mesh. This Kelly rapidly adjusted over my head. The only explanation that I can find for my submitting so tamely to all this is that Spooky Byrne must have possessed hypnotic powers.

Anyhow, I sat in that chair, which was comfortable enough. I watched Kelly fussing around with the Mannschenn Drive controls while Byrne did things to his own console—which looked more like an aquarium in which luminous, insubstantial, formless fish were swimming than anything else. The drive rotors started to turn, to spin, to precess. I wanted to close my eyes; after all, it is dinned into us from boyhood up never to look directly at the Mannschenn Drive in operation. I wanted to close my eyes, but couldn't. I watched those blasted, shimmering wheels spinning, tumbling, fading, always on the verge of invisibility but ever pulsatingly a-glimmer. . . .

I listened to the familiar thin, high whine of the machine. . . .

That sound persisted; otherwise the experience was like watching one of those ancient silent films in an entertainments museum. There was no other noise, although that of the Drive unit could almost have come from an archaic projector. There were no smells, no sensations. There were just pictures mostly out of focus and with the colors not quite right. But I saw Kelly—the here-and-now Kelly, not his villainous ancestor—recognizable in spite of the full beard that he was wearing, in some sort of sumptuous regalia, a golden crown in which emeralds gleamed set on his head. And there was Byrne, more soberly but still richly attired, reminding me somehow of the legendary wizard Merlin who was the power behind King Arthur's throne. And there were glimpses of a flag, a glowing green banner with a golden harp in the upper canton, the stars of the Southern Cross, also in gold, on the fly. And I saw myself. It was me, all right. I was wearing a green uniform with gold braid up to the elbows. The badge on my cap, with its bullion-encrusted peak, was a golden crown over a winged, golden harp. . . .

The lights went out, came on again. I was sitting in the chair looking at the motionless machine, at Kelly and Byrne, who were looking at me.

Kelly said, "There are crucial points in history. The 'ifs' of history. *If* Napoleon had accepted Fulton's offer of steamships . . . just imagine a squadron of steam frigates at Trafalgar! *If* Pickett's charge at Gettysburg had been successful . . . *If* Admiral Torrance had met the Waverley Navy head on off New Dunedine instead of despatching his forces in a fruitless chase of Commodore McWhirter and his raiding squadron.

"And . . .

"*If* Thomas Curnow had not succeeded in flagging down the special train before it reached Glenrowan.

"You've seen what could have been, what can be. The extrapolation. Myself king. Spooky my chief minister. You—an admiral."

I laughed. In spite of what I'd just seen it still seemed absurd. "All right," I said. "You might be king. But why should I be an admiral?"

He said, "It could be a sort of hereditary rank granted, in the first instance, to that ancestor of yours for services rendered. When you're fighting a war at the end of long lines of supply somebody on your staff who knows about ships is useful—"

"I've looked," said Spooky Byrne. "I've seen how things were after the massacre of the police outside Glenrowan. I've seen the rising of the poor, the oppressed, spreading from Victoria to New South Wales, under the flag of the Golden Harp and Southern Cross. I've seen the gunboats on the Murray, the armored paddlewheelers with their steam-powered Gatling canon, an' the armored trains ranging up an' down the countryside. An' it was yourself, Grimes—or your ancestor—who put to good use the supplies that were comin' in from our Fenian brothers in America an' even from the German emperor. I've watched the Battle of Port Phillip Bay—the English warships an' troop transports, with the Pope's Eye battery wreakin' havoc among 'em until a lucky shot found its magazine. An' then your flimsy gasbags came a-sailin' over, droppin' their bombs, an' not a gun could be brought to bear on 'em. . . ."

"Airships?" I demanded. "You certainly have been seeing things, Spooky!"

"Yes, airships. There was a man called Bland in Sydney, somethin' of a rebel himself, who designed an airship years before Ned was ever heard of. An' you—or your ancestor—could have found those plans. You, in your ancestor's mind, sort of nudgin'—just as Eddie an' meself 'll be doing our own nudgin' . . ."

I wasn't quite sober so, in spite of my protestations, what Spooky was saying, combined with what I had seen, seemed to make sense. So when Kelly said that we should now, all three of us, return to the past, to the year 1880, old reckoning, I did not object. I realized dimly that they had been expecting me, waiting for me. That they were needing me. I must have been an obnoxious puppy in those days—but aren't we all when still wet behind the ears? I actually thought of bargaining. A dukedom on top of the admiral's commission . . . the Duke of Alice . . . ? It sounded good.

Kelly and Byrne were seated now, one on either side of me. There were controls set in the armrests of their chairs. Lattice-work skeps, like the one that I was wearing, were over their heads. The rotors started to spin, to spin and precess, glimmering, fading, tumbling, dragging our *essences* down the dark dimensions while our bodies remained solidly seated in the here and now.

§ § §

I listened to the familiar thin, high whine of the machine. . . .

To the babble of rough voices, male and female. . . . To the piano-accordion being not too inexpertly played . . . An Irish song it was—"The Wearin' of the Green" . . . I smelled tobacco smoke, the fumes of beer and of strong liquor. . . . I opened my eyes and looked around me. It was *real*—far more real than the unconvincing reconstruction in the here-and-now Glenrowan had been. The slatternly women were a far cry from those barmaids tarted up in allegedly period costume. And here there were no tourists, gaily dressed and hung around with all manner of expensive recording equipment. Here were burly, bearded, roughclad men and it was weapons, antique revolvers, that they carried, not the very latest trivoders.

But the group of men of whom I was one were not armed. They were laborers, not bushrangers—but they looked up to the arrogant giant who was holding forth just as much as did his fellow . . . criminals? Yes, they were that. They had held up coaches, robbed banks, murdered. Yet to these Irish laborers he was a hero, a deliverer. He stood for the Little Man against the Establishment. He stood for a warmly human religion against one whose priests were never recruited from the ranks of the ordinary people, the peasants, the workers.

Mind you, I was seeing him through the eyes of that ancestral Grimes who was (temporarily) a criminal himself, who was (temporarily) a rebel, who was on the run (he thought) from the forces of Law and Order. I had full access to his memories. I was, more or less, him. More or less, I say. Nonetheless, I, Grimes the spaceman, was a guest in the mind of Grimes the seaman. I could remember that quarrel on the poop of the *Lady Lucan* and how Captain Jenkins, whose language was always foul, had excelled himself, calling me what was, in those days, an impossibly vile epithet. I lost my temper, Jenkins lost a few teeth, and I lost my job, hastily leaving the ship in Melbourne before Jenkins could have me arrested on a charge of mutiny on the high seas.

And now, mainly because of the circumstances in which I found myself, I was on the point of becoming one of those middle class technicians who, through the ages, have thrown in their lot with charismatic rebel leaders, without whom those same alleged deliverers of the oppressed masses would have gotten no place at all. I—*now*—regard with abhorrence the idea of derailing a special train on the way to apprehend a rather vicious criminal. That ancestral Grimes, in his later years, must have felt the same sentiments—so much so that he never admitted to anybody that he was among those present at the Siege of Glenrowan.

But Ned Kelly is. . . . He was in good form, although there was something odd about him. He seemed to be . . . possessed. So was the man—Joe Byrne—standing beside him. And so, of course, was John Grimes, lately second mate of the good ship *Lady Lucan*. Kelly—which Kelly?—must have realized that he was drawing some odd looks from his adherents. He broke the tension by putting on his famous helmet—the sheet-iron cylinder with only a slit for the eyes—and singing while he was wearing it. This drew both laughter and applause. Did you ever see those singing robots that were quite a craze a few years back? The effect was rather similar. Great art it was not but it was good for a laugh.

Nobody saw the schoolmaster, Thomas Curnow, sneaking out but me. That was rather odd as he, fancying himself a cut above the others making merry in the hotel, had been keeping himself to himself, saying little, drinking sparingly. This should have made him conspicuous but, somehow, it had the reverse effect. He was the outsider, being studiously ignored. I tried to attract Kelly's attention, Byrne's attention, but I might as well just not have been there. After all I—or my host—was an outsider too. I was the solitary Englishman among the Australians and the Irish. The gang with whom I'd been working on the railway had never liked me. The word had gotten around that I was an officer. The fact that I was (temporarily, as it happened) an ex-officer made no difference. I was automatically suspect.

But I still wanted to be an admiral. I still wanted to command those squadrons of gunboats on the Murray River, the air fleet that would turn the tide at Port Phillip Bay. (How much of my inward voice was the rum speaking, how much was me? How much did the John Grimes whose brain I was taking over ever know about it, remember about it?)

I followed Curnow, out into the cold, clear night. The railway track was silvery in the light of the lopsided moon, near its meridian. On either side, dark and ominous, was the bush. Some nocturnal bird or animal called out, a raucous cry, and something else answered it. And faint—but growing louder—there was a sort of chuffing rattle coming up from the south'ard. The pilot engine, I thought, and then the special train.

Ahead of me Curnow's lantern, a yellow star where no star should have been, was bobbing along between the tracks. I remembered the story. He had the lantern, and his wife's red scarf. He would wave them. The train would stop. Superintendent Hare, Inspector O'Connor, the white troopers, and the black trackers would pile out. And then the shooting, and the siege, and the fire, and that great, armored figure, like some humanoid robot before its time, stumbling out through the smoke and the flame for the final showdown with his enemies.

And it was up to me to change the course of history.

Have you ever tried walking along a railway line, especially when you're in something of a hurry? The sleepers or the ties or whatever they're called are spaced at just the wrong distance for a normal human stride. Curnow was doing better than I was. Well, he was more used to it. Neither as a seaman nor as a spaceman had I ever had occasion to take a walk such as this.

And then—he fell. He'd tripped, I suppose. He'd fallen with such force as to knock himself out. When I came up to him I found that he'd tried to save that precious lantern from damage. It was on its side but the chimney was unbroken, although one side of the glass was blackened by the smoke from the burning oil.

And the train was coming. I could see it now—the glaring yellow headlight of the leading locomotive, the orange glow from the fireboxes, a shower of sparks mingling with the smoke from the funnels. I had to get Curnow off the line. I tried to lift him but one foot was somehow jammed under the sleeper over

which he had tripped. But his lantern, as I have already said, was still burning. I hastily turned it to the right side up; only one side of the chimney was smoked into opacity. And that flimsy, translucent red scarf was still there.

I lifted the lantern, held it so that the colored fabric acted as a filter. I waved it—not fast, for fear that the light would be blown out, but slowly, deliberately. The train, the metal monster, kept on coming. I knew that I'd soon have to look after myself but was determined to stand there until the last possible second.

The whistle of the leading locomotive, the pilot engine, sounded—a long, mournful note. There was a screaming of brakes, a great, hissing roar of escaping steam, shouting . . .

I realized that Curnow had recovered, had scrambled to his feet, was standing beside me. I thrust the lantern and the scarf into his hand, ran into the bushes at the side of the track. He could do all the explaining. I—or that ancestral Grimes—had no desire to meet the police. For all I—or *he*—knew they would regard the capture of a mutineer and deserter as well as a gang of bushrangers as an unexpected bonus.

I stayed in my hiding place—cold, bewildered, more than a little scared. After a while I heard the shooting, the shouting and the screaming. I saw the flames. I was too far away to see Ned Kelly's last desperate stand; all that I observed was distant, shadowy figures in silhouette against the burning hotel.

Suddenly, without warning, I was back in my chair in that other Kelly's laboratory. The machine, the modified Mannschenn Drive unit, had stopped. I looked at Byrne. I knew, without examining him, that he, too, had . . . stopped. Kelly was alive but not yet fully conscious. His mouth was working. I could just hear what he was muttering; "It had to come to this." And those, I recalled, had been the last words of Ned Kelly, the bushranger, just before they hanged him.

I reasoned, insofar as I was capable of reasoning, that Kelly and Byrne had entered too deeply into the minds of their criminal ancestors. Joe Byrne had died in the siege and his descendant had died with him. Kelly had been badly wounded, although he recovered sufficiently to stand trial. I'd been lucky enough to escape almost unscathed.

I'm not at all proud of what I did then. I just got up and left them—the dead man, his semi-conscious cousin. I got out of there, fast. When I left the Glenrowan Tower I took a cab to the airport and there bought a ticket on the first flight out of the city. It was going to Perth, a place that I'd never much wanted to visit, but at least it was putting distance between me and the scene of that hapless experiment, that presumptuous attempt at tinkering with Time.

I've often wondered what would have happened if I'd left Curnow to his fate, if I hadn't stopped the train. The course of history might well have been changed—but would it have been for the better? I don't think so. An Irish Australia, a New Erin, a Harp in the South . . . New Erin allied with the Boers against hated England during the wars in South Africa . . . New Erin quite possibly allied with Germany against England during the First World War . . . The Irish, in many ways, are a great people—but they carry a grudge to absurd lengths. They have far too long a memory for their own wrongs.

And I think that I like me better as I am now than as an Hereditary Admiral of the New Erin Navy in an alternate universe that, fortunately, didn't happen.

§ § §

She said, "Thank you, Commodore, for a very interesting story." She switched off her trivoder, folded flat its projections, closed the carrying case about it. She got to her feet. She said, "I have to be going."

He looked at the bulkhead clock. He said, "There's no hurry, Kitty. We've time for another drink or two." He sensed a coldness in the atmosphere and tried to warm things up with an attempt at humor. "Sit down again. Make yourself comfortable. This ship is Liberty Hall, you know. You can spit on that mat and call the cat a bastard."

She said, "The only tom cats I've seen aboard this wagon haven't been of the four-legged variety. And, talking of legs, do you think that I haven't noticed the way that you've been eyeing mine?"

His prominent ears reddened angrily but he persisted. "Will you be at the cocktail party tonight?"

"No, Commodore Grimes. Station Yorick isn't interested in boring social functions."

"But I'll be seeing more of you, I hope. . . ."

"You will not, in either sense of the words." She turned to go. "You said, Commodore, that the Irish have a long memory for their own wrongs. Perhaps you are right. Be that as it may—you might be interested to learn that my family name is Kelly."

When she was gone Grimes reflected wryly that now there was yet another alternate universe, differing from his here-and-now only in a strictly personal sense, which he would never enter.

THE THIRD DR. MOREAU
by Martin Gardner

Here is a multiple puzzle from Mr. Gardner that is set on Earth. The author's latest book, Mathematical Magic Show, *was recently published by Knopf; it includes a witty, 22-entry dictionary of some of the more esoteric mathematical terms.*

It is not widely known among science fiction buffs that Dr. Moreau, about whom H. G. Wells wrote his famous SF novella, had a grandson who calls himself Dr. Moreau III. Dr. Moreau III is a professor of genetics at King's College, in London, where he is considered one of the world's top researchers in genetic engineering.

By tinkering with a microbe's DNA helix, Dr. Moreau III recently managed to produce a strange new type of one-celled organism which he calls *septolis quarkolis*. Drawing nourishment from the air and using energy derived from quarks, the new microbe splits every hour into seven replicas of itself. Each replica instantly becomes the same size as the original. Thus after one hour a single microbe becomes seven, after another hour the seven become 49, in another hour the 49 become 343, and so on. As Dr. Moreau put it, in his report in *Nature, septolis quarkolis* "multiplies at an alarming rate."

One day Dr. Moreau III put a single microbe, just "born," into a large and empty glass container. Fifty hours later the container was completely filled. Dr. Moreau then quickly destroyed all the microbes by bombarding them with tachyons. Otherwise, in a few more days they would have engulfed all of King's College.

I happened to be visiting King's College a few days after this event. Always alert for puzzle possibilities,

I asked Dr. Moreau III's assistant, a chimpanzee named Montgomery, when the glass container was exactly 1/7 full of the microbes. Montgomery whipped out his pocket calculator and started working on the problem, but an hour later he still didn't have the answer. It was, he told me, beyond the capacity of his computer's readout.

Can the reader determine how many hours elapsed until the container was 1/7 full? See page 79 for the answer.

THE SMALL STONES OF TU FU

by Brian W. Aldiss

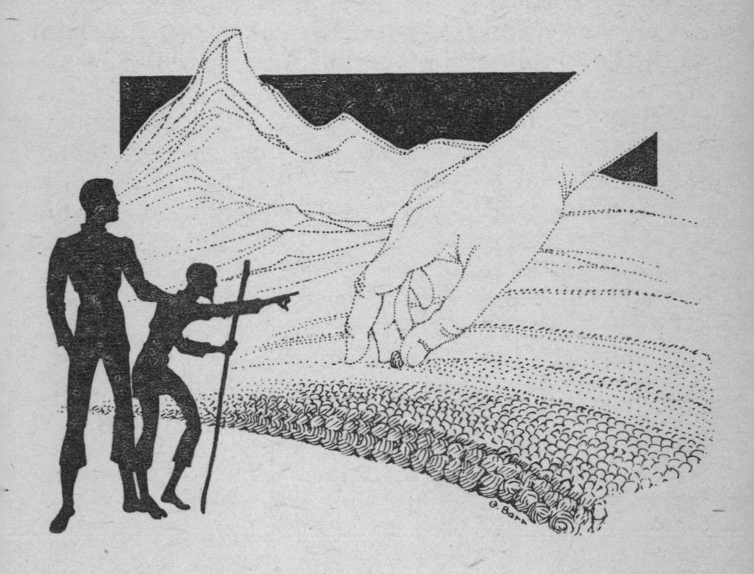

The author has been writing and selling SF at an enviable rate since his first sale, which appeared in 1954. British by birth and current residence, Mr. Aldiss describes himself as in the travel belt: after Poland, Czechoslovakia, and Ireland in 1976, he visited the U.S.S.R. as a guest of the Soviet Writers' Union, and is now preparing for trips to Scandinavia and Italy. He still hopes to get to China one day, the setting of this unclassifiable tale.

On the 20th day of the Fifth Month of Year V of Ta-li (which would be May in A.D. 770, according to the Old Christian calendar), I was taking a voyage down the Yangtse River with the aged poet Tu Fu.

Tu Fu was withered even then. Yet his words, and the spaces between his words, will never wither. As a person, Tu Fu was the most civilised and musing man I ever met, which explains my long stay in that epoch. Ever since then, I have wondered whether the art of being amusing, with its implied detachment from self, is not one of the most undervalued requisites of human civilization. In many epochs, being amusing is equated with triviality. The human race rarely understood what was important; but Tu Fu understood.

Although the sage was ill, and little more than a bag of bones, he desired to visit White King again before he died.

"Though I fear that the mere apparition of my skinny self at a place named White King," he said, "may be sufficient for that apparition, the White Knight, to make his last move on me."

It is true that white is the Chinese colour of mourning, but I wondered if a pun could prod the spirits into action; were they so sensitive to words?

"What can a spirit digest but words?" Tu Fu replied. "I don't entertain the idea that spirits can eat or drink—though one hears of them whining at keyholes. They are forced to lead a tediously spiritual life." He chuckled.

This was even pronounced with spirit, for poor Tu Fu had recently been forced to give up drinking. When I mentioned that sort of spirit, he said "Yes, I linger on life's balcony, ill and alone, and must not drink for fear I fall off."

Here again, I sensed that his remark was detached and not self-pitying, as some might construe it; his compassion was with all who aged and who faced death before they were ready—although, as Tu Fu himself remarked, "If we were not forced to go until we were ready, the world would be mountain-deep with the ill-prepared." I could but laugh at his turn of phrase.

When the Yangtse boat drew in to the jetty at White King, I helped the old man ashore. This was what we had come to see: the great white stones which progressed out of the swirling river and climbed its shores, the last of the contingent standing grandly in the soil of a tilled field.

I marvelled at the energy Tu Fu displayed. Most of the other passengers flocked round a refreshment-vendor who set up his pitch upon the shingle, or else climbed a belvedere to view the landscape at ease. The aged poet insisted on walking among the monoliths.

"When I first visited this district as a young scholar, many years ago," said Tu Fu, as we stood looking up at the great bulk towering over us, "I was naturally curious as to the origin of these stones. I sought out the clerk in the district office and enquired of him. He said, 'The god called the Great Archer shot the stones out of the sky. That is one explanation. They were set there by a great king to commemorate the fact that the waters of the Yangtse flow East. That is another explanation. They were purely accidental. That is a third explanation.' So I asked him which of these explanations he personally subscribed to, and he replied, 'Why, young fellow, I wisely subscribe to all three, and shall continue to do so until more plausible explanations are offered.' Can you imagine a situation in which caution and credulity, *coupled with extreme scepticism,* were more nicely combined?" We both laughed.

"I'm sure your clerk went far."

"No doubt. He had moved to the adjacent room even before I left his office. For a long while, I used to wonder about his statement that a great king had commemorated the fact that the Yangtse waters flowed East; I could only banish the idiocy from my mind by writing a poem about it."

I laughed. Remembrance dawned. I quoted it to him.

"I need no knot in my robe
To remember the Lady Li's kisses;
Small kings commemorate rivers
And are themselves forgotten."

"There is real pleasure in poetry," responded Tu Fu, "when spoken so beautifully and remembered so appositely. But you had to be prompted."

"I was prompt to deliver, sir."

We walked about the monoliths, watching the waters swirl and curdle and fawn round the base of a giant stone as they made their way through the gorges of the Yangtse down to the ocean. Tu Fu said that he believed the monoliths to be a memorial set there by Chu-Ko Liang, demonstrating a famous tactical disposition by which he had won many battles during the wars of the Three Kingdoms.

"Are your reflections profound at moments like this?" Tu Fu asked, after a pause, and I reflected how rare it was to find a man, whether young or old, who was genuinely interested in the thoughts of others.

"What with the solidity of the stone and the ceaseless mobility of the water, I feel they should be profound. Instead, my mind is obstinately blank."

"Come, come," he said chidingly, "the river is moving too fast for you to expect any reflection. Now if it were still water. . ."

"It is still water even when it is moving fast, sir."

"There I must give you best, or give you up. But, pray, look at the gravels here and tell me what you observe. I am interested to know if we see the same things."

Something in his manner told me that more was expected of me than jokes. I looked along the shore, where stones of all kinds were distributed, from sand and grits to stones the size of a man's head, according to the disposition of current and tide.

"I confess I see nothing striking. The scene is a familiar one, although I have never been here before. You might come upon a little beach like this on any tidal river, or along the coasts by the Yellow Sea."

Looking at him in puzzlement, I saw he was staring out across the flood, although he had confessed he saw little in the distance nowadays. Because I sensed the knowledge stirring in him, my role of innocent had to be played more determinedly than ever.

"Many thousands of people come to this spot every year," he said. "They come to marvel at Chu-Ko Liang's giant stones, which are popularly known as 'The Eight Formations,' by the way. Of course, what is big is indeed marvellous, and the act of marvelling is very satisfying to the emotions, provided one is not called upon to do it every day of the year. But I marvel now, as I did when I first found myself on this spot, at a different thing. I marvel at the stones on the shore."

A light breeze was blowing, and for a moment I held in my nostrils the whiff of something appetising, a crab-and-ginger soup perhaps, warming at the food-vendor's fire further down the beach, where our boat was moored. Greed awoke a faint impatience in me, so that I thought, before humans are old, they should pamper their poor dear bodies, for the substance wastes away before the spirit, and was vexed to imagine that I had guessed what Tu Fu was going to say before he spoke. I was sorry to think that he might confess to being impressed by mere numbers. But his next remark surprised me.

"We marvel at the giant stones because they are unaccountable. We should rather marvel at the little ones because they are accountable. Let us walk upon them." I fell in with him and we paced over them: first a troublesome bank of grit, which grew larger on the seaward side of the bank. Then a patch of almost bare sand. Then, abruptly, shoals of pebbles, the individual members of which grew larger until we were confronted with a pile of lumpy stones which Tu

Fu did not attempt to negotiate. We went round it, to find ourselves on more sand, followed by well-rounded stones all the size of a man's clenched fist. And they in turn gave way to more grit. Our discomfort in walking—which Tu Fu overcame in part by resting an arm on my arm—was increased by the fact that these divisions of stones were made not only laterally along the beach but vertically up the beach, the demarcations in the latter division being frequently marked by lines of seaweed or of minute white shells of dead crustaceans.

"Enough, if not more than enough," said Tu Fu. "Now do you see what is unusual about the beach?"

"I confess I find it a tiresomely *usual* beach," I replied, masking my thoughts.

"You observe how all the stones are heaped according to their size."

"That too is usual, sir. You will ask me to marvel next that students in classrooms appear to be graded according to size."

"Ha!" He stood and peered up at me, grinning and stroking his long white beard. "But we agree that students are graded according to the wishes of the teacher. Now, according to whose wishes are all these millions upon millions of pebbles graded?"

"Wishes don't enter into it. The action of the water is sufficient, the action of the water, working ceaselessly and randomly. The playing, one may say, of the inorganic organ."

Tu Fu coughed and wiped the spittle from his thin lips.

"Although you claim to be born in the remote future, which I confess seems to me unnatural, you are familiar with the workings of this natural world. So, like most people, you see nothing marvellous in the stones hereabouts. Supposing you were born—" he paused and looked about him and upwards, as far as the infirmity of his years would allow— "supposing you were born upon the moon, which some sages claim is a dead world, bereft of life, women, and wine. . . . If you then flew to this world and, in girdling it, observed everywhere stones, arranged in sizes as these are here. Wherever you travelled, by the coasts of any sea, you saw that the stones of the world had been arranged in sizes. What then would you think?"

I hesitated—Tu Fu was too near for comfort.

"I believe my thoughts would turn to crab-and-ginger soup, sir."

"No, they would not, not if you came from the moon, which is singularly devoid of crab-and-ginger soup, if reports speak true. You would be forced to the conclusion, the inevitable conclusion, that the stones of this world were being graded, like your scholars, by a superior intelligence." He turned the collar of his padded coat up against the breeze, which was freshening. "You would come to believe that that Intelligence was obsessive, that its mind was terrible indeed, filled only with the idea—not of language, which is human—but of number, which is inhuman. You would understand of that Intelligence that it was under an interdict to wander the world measuring and weighing every one of a myriad myriad single stones, sorting them all into heaps according to dimension. Meaningless heaps, heaps without even particular decorative merit. The farther you travelled, the more heaps you saw—the myriad heaps, each containing myriads of stones—the more alarmed you would become. And what would you conclude in the end?"

Laughing with some anger, I said, "That it was better to stay at home."

"Possibly. You would also conclude that it was *no use* staying at home. Because the Intelligence that haunted the earth was interested only in stones; that you would perceive. From which it would follow that the Intelligence would be hostile to anything else and, in particular, would be hostile to anything which disturbed its handiwork."

"Such as human kind?"

"Precisely." He pointed up the strand, where our fellow-voyagers were sitting on the shingle, or kicking it about, while their children were pushing stones into piles or flinging them into the Yangtse. "The Intelligence—diligent, obsessive, methodical to a degree—would come in no time to be especially weary of human kind, who were busy turning what is ordered into what is random."

Thinking that he was beginning to become alarmed by his own fancy, I said, "It is a good subject for a poem, perhaps, but nothing more. Let us return to the boat. I see the sailors are going aboard."

We walked along the beach, taking care not to disturb the stones. Tu Fu coughed as he walked.

"So you believe that what I say about the Intelligence that haunts the earth is nothing more than a fit subject for a poem?" he said. He stopped slowly to pick up a stone, fitting his other hand in the small of his back in order to regain an upright posture. We both stood and looked at it as it lay in Tu Fu's withered palm. No man had a name for its precise shape, or even for the fugitive tints of cream and white and black which marked it out as different from all its neighbours. Tu Fu stared down at it and improvised an epigram.

"The stone in my hand hides
A secret natural history:
Climates and times unknown,
A river unseen."

I held my hand out. "You don't know it, but you have released that stone from the bondage of space and time. May I keep it?"

As he passed it over, and we stepped towards the refreshment-vendor, Tu Fu said, more lightly, "We take foul medicines to improve our health; so we must entertain foul thoughts on occasion, to strengthen wisdom. Can you nourish no belief in my Intelligence—you, who claim to be born in some remote future—which loves stones but hates human kind? Do I claim too much to ask you to suppose for a moment that I might be correct in my supposition? . . ." Evidently his thought wandered slightly, for he then said, after a pause, "Is it within the power of one man to divine the secret nature of the world, or is even the whisper of that wish a supreme egotism, punishable by a visitation from the White Knight?"

"Permit me to get you a bowl of soup, sir."

The vendor provided us with two mats to lay over the shingle. We unrolled them and sat to drink our crab-and-ginger soup. As he supped, with the drooling noises of an old man, the sage gazed far away down the restless river, where lantern sails moved distantly towards the sea, yellow on the yellow skyline. His previously cheerful, even playful, mood had slipped from him; I could perceive that, at his advanced age, even the yellow distance might be a reminder to him—perhaps as much reassuring as painful—that he soon must himself journey to a great distance. I recited his epigram to myself. "Climates and times unknown, A river unseen."

Children played round us. Their parents, moving slowly up the gangplank on to the vessel, called to them. "Did you like the giant stones, venerable master?" one of the boys asked Tu Fu, cheekily.

"I like them better than the battles they commemorate," replied Tu Fu. He stretched out a papery hand, and patted the boy's shoulder before the latter ran after his father. I had remarked before the way in which the aged long to touch the young.

We also climbed the gangplank. It was a manifest effort for Tu Fu.

Dark clouds were moving from the interior, dappling the landscape with moving shadow. I took Tu Fu below, to rest in a little cabin we had hired for the journey. He sat on the bare bench, in stoical fashion, breathing flutteringly, while I thought of the battle to which he referred, which I had paused to witness some centuries earlier.

Just above our heads, the bare feet of the crew pattered on the deck. There was a prolonged creaking as the gangplank was hoisted, followed by the rattle of the sail unfolding. The wind caught the boat, every plank of which responded to that exhalation, and we started to glide forward with the Yangtse's great stone-shaping course towards the sea. A harmony of motion caused the whole ship to come alive, every separate part of it rubbing against every other, as in the internal workings of a human when it runs.

I turned to Tu Fu. His eyes went blank, his jaw fell open. One hand moved to clutch his beard and then fell away. He toppled forward—I managed to catch him before he struck the floor. In my arms, he seemed to weigh nothing. A muttered word broke from him, then a heavy shuddering sigh.

The White Knight had come, Tu Fu's spirit was gone. I laid him upon the bench, looking down at his revered form with compassion. Then I climbed up on deck.

There the crowd of travellers was standing at the starboard side, watching the tawny coast roll by, and crying out with some excitement. But they fell silent, facing me attentively when I called to them.

"Friends," I shouted. "The great and beloved poet Tu Fu is dead."

A first sprinkle of rain fell from the west, and the sun became hidden by cloud.

§ § §

Swimming strongly on my way back to what the sage called the remote future, my form began to flow and change according to time pressure. Sometimes my essence was like steam, sometimes like a mountain. Always I clung to the stone I had taken from Tu Fu's hand.

Back. Finally I was back. Back was an enormous expanse yet but a corner. All human kind had long departed. All life had disappeared. Only the great organ of the inorganic still played. There I could sit on my world-embracing beach, eternally arranging and grading pebble after pebble. From fine grit to great boulders, they could all be sorted as I desired. In that occupation, I fulfilled the pleasures of infinity, for it was inexhaustible.

But the small stone of Tu Fu I kept apart. Of all beings ever to exist upon the bounteous face of this world, Tu Fu had been nearest to me—I say "had been," but he forever *is*, and I return to visit him when I will. For it was he who came nearest to understanding my existence by pure divination.

Even his comprehension failed. He needed to take his perceptions a stage further and see how those same natural forces which create stones also create human beings. The Intelligence that haunts the earth is not hostile to human beings. Far from it—I regard them with the same affection as I do the smallest pebble.

Why, take this little pebble at my side! I never saw a pebble like that before. The tint of this facet, here—isn't that unique?

I have a special bank on which to store it, somewhere over the other side of the world. Only the little stone of Tu Fu shall not be stored away; small kings commemorate rivers, and this stone shall commemorate the immortal river of Tu Fu's thought.

A HIDEOUS SPLOTCH OF PURPLE

by Theresa Harned

The author reports that, in the past two years, she has written at least ten stories, none of which ever got finished, before one was produced above the aauggh level; she is threatening to take another look at some of the monsters now stacked away. She is 36, a native of California with a background in the biological sciences. After a mixed bag of occupations, she is now in the business of selling options in the commodity market.

I think I've been had. Nah, let's put that another way. I know I've been had and maybe, just maybe you've been had too. Look, before I get into this, a cup of black coffee would be nice so hold everything while I fix one. I take mine instant. You may never create a great cup of coffee but the taste will always be the same.

Where was I? Oh yeah, about where I thought. Well, mornings I usually make business calls. An art gallery doesn't survive without outside selling. While I'm out, Charlie, who looks like a Greek god with muscles he'll never use except for the benefit of the barbell set, watches the shop. He's the kind who reads *People Magazine* for intellectual stimulation. He opens up by nineish and waits around until I arrive, usually by twoish.

This Thursday was special because a big British bank had agreed to display a selection of our artists' work. I was floating along six inches above the sidewalk by the time I got to the gallery. Even the vacant smile Charlie wore didn't irritate me.

"How's business?" I said as I always do when I come in from the morning's war.

"Some guy wants that one." Charlie pointed to the ugliest oil hanging in the gallery. I stopped paralyzed with shock.

"Somebody wants to buy POKER BOY?" Incredible. Charlie was getting his coat on preparatory to leaving. As usual there was a lot of personal business that needed his immediate attention.

"Yeah." He whipped out a pocket brush and ran it through the blond shag around his face. "He wanted to talk to the owner so I guess he'll be back later."

"When is later? Today, tomorrow?" Control yourself, kid.

"Don't know. Bye now." Charlie vanished, moving as fast as he would all day. Poker Boy was probably the grossest oil I had ever agreed to hang. The only reason it was there in all its uggh was that Sheila, who did it, called on me to repay a favor. True, she had helped me get started ten years ago. Her style hadn't improved any. Still at odds with the whole human race, everything she committed came out in garish red-orange on midnight purple. This particular monstrosity someone totally out of touch wanted was a portrait of a hermaphrodite. Sprawled across the canvas, knobby muscles, stringy limbs splayed at random, it was as awful as ever.

I settled down at the small desk beside the entrance. This big roomy place of light was friendly (in spite of puke boy). A lot of sweat had gone into bringing it up to standard. Too bad I was going to lose it if next month's rent didn't materialize from somewhere. With any luck, the bank would come through. Gallery business is iffy as are all artistic endeavors. There's so much competition. One month in six you're lucky to do well enough to carry you over the next dry spell. We needed a big sale, but then we always needed a big sale. Incidentally I could use a trifle for eats and to pay the electric bill. And would it be asking too much for an extra fifty bucks to put out a catalogue mailing.

All these worries ran through my mind while I was putting the house business in order. There wasn't much. A few unserious people wandered through. Along about 4 o'clock I was ready for *People Magazine*. I had actually taken it from Charlie's drawer when a shadow fell across me. Somehow, I knew. Maybe it was the way he looked through me or the feeling that passed between us—me entomologist, you insect.

"Hello, I'm Manfred Cady," his hollow voice startled me. "Are you the owner?" Manfred spoke with no regional accent. I'm pretty good on dialects, not as skilled as an etymologist, but I can tell a Tennessean from a Kentuckian and a coastal Georgia twang from an Alabama argot. Cady spoke perfect standard American, of which there is no such thing. Every word was a network news-speak average. I'd never heard anyone talk that way before. It was dead English and it made me itchy. I wanted to shake him up.

"You're right on two counts," I said. "Your name is Cady and I'm the owner of this place of business." I handed him my conservative chocolate-on-beige business card.

"Thank you." Handling it like a clue at a crime, he slipped it into a plastic holder crowded with bright advertising gimmicks. That bit of formality completed he headed straight for Putrid Boy. I followed him over. He got right down to business. "How much are you asking?"

My mind was into sixth gear. Could this character be for real? Ideas flashed by like butterflies in a high wind. I dismissed them as fast as they suggested themselves.

"The artist is Sheila Savage." Two theories surfaced. One, he was a foreign agent just out of agent school trying out his English on unsuspecting Americanski, not good; two, alien from another planet (star system?) trying out his English on unsuspecting native lifeform, even worse.

"I would like to purchase it."

"Why that's just wonderful. I'm sure Sheila will be pleased as punch." Sarcasm was lost on this turkey. Had he not been so set on buying I might have made him an offer—here fella, five bucks to take this thing away. No, ridiculous, shut up. Sheila would never forgive me.

"The price is one thousand dollars."

"When may I take delivery?" He was as straight as a narc at a Republican fund raiser.

Wow. "Well, methinks the present is as good a time as any, providing, of course, you have the money."

Cady's eyes returned to the painting. "Would you deliver it?"

"Sure." For $1,000 I'd carry it to Elko, Nevada, on a bicycle, nude with a rose behind each ear. Sheila would be delighted and want to place more "paintings" with me. I waited. He could not seem to get enough of Poker Boy. At last he pulled himself away.

"I have travelers' checks. Will they be acceptable?"

I nodded. "Anything with pictures that I can pass on to an unsuspecting public. You have I.D.?"

"I.D.?" An eyebrow quivered.

You just failed Idiomatic English 102, I thought.

"Like, driver's license, passport, work card, credit cards . . ."

"Oh, of course." He pulled out a regular California driver's license which I looked at very closely. In the meantime he began signing Chase Manhattan travelers' checks. Five twenties. I bet he was a traveler, eight fifties. According to his driver's license he lived in San Francisco. Now he was into the hundred buck checks. It didn't seem logical (how I hate that word) to buy and use travelers' checks in the same city you lived in. Strange people do strange things. Shit. He's from San Francisco like I'm from Moscow, Idaho, I argued. But why carp? Chase guaranteed their paper. Cady straightened up. I flipped through his checks, all signed in conservative blue ink.

"As to delivery, the address is here." He handed me a slick piece of plastic.

"When?"

"As soon as possible."

"That'd be tomorrow morning around nineish."

"Thank you. I'll be waiting for you." Cady exited. What self control. He didn't once glance back.

§ § §

Bright and early Charlie carefully stowed the six-by-seven-foot crate, with much flexion and definition of muscular torso, in the back of my van. We made the South San Francisco area in good time. It was one of those typical mornings, cool and foggy, damp and still. The late morning wind had not yet sprung up to blow the stuff away, and the sun's rays hadn't had enough time to burn their way through the overcast. Eventually we'd be treated to a sparkling deep blue sky, a few wispy cloudlets, and crying gulls riding windswept grit.

We came to an area deteriorating even by south-of-Market standards. Weed-filled lots overflowed onto crumbling sidewalks. Looking like toothless faces, broken-windowed buildings bordered fix-it shops, secondhand stores, and dirty little garages. This was where the immaculately outfitted Cady had his office? The number on his card matched that on a corrugated tin warehouse. Rust-streaked siding met caches of rubbish at its base. Cady had paid a thousand bucks for a piece of canvas and here his place of business looked like something that had barely survived the great quake. I backed the van up to the sliding door in front. Charlie trotted out and pounded on the scaly metal door inset. I briefly considered the idea that Manfred had given us a bogus address for some weird reason. But he must have been waiting because the door, the big sliding door that is, slowly rolled open. Standing in the middle was Cady. Fog swirled about him and combined with the gloom of the interior to give him a vaguely threatening appearance. He broke the mood immediately by walking over to the rear of the van. Same suit, same expression, a hash of reserve and hauteur. Hellos all around, we exchanged minimal greetings. Part of me wanted to be brief and businesslike. However, curiosity and my boiling imagination held my mouth hostage and were making demands.

Casually I said, "Do you mind?" I motioned to Charlie to start unloading. "We like to deliver our artwork space to place. Just show us where to put it." I wanted to see the inside of that barn.

"Certainly, this way please." He didn't sound as sure as he pretended to be. Maybe I was getting through. Heh, heh. We bracketed the crate, hefted, and followed Cady's rapidly dissolving figure. To say that details were difficult to make out would not be correct. It was goddam dark in there, so dark that we could barely see where we were going. I couldn't make out an elephant should one have been two feet from me unless he had halitosis—only jumbled impressions of crowded aisles, boxes heaped above us, hemming us in. Like native bearers in a grade B movie, we followed bwana deep into the guts of the beast. The little light available was reflected from Cady's flowing figure. Somehow he had produced a small pocket flash. He stopped, indicating a space amongst the rank upon rank of bulky shrouded objects. I was so busy looking around that I almost ran into him.

"Sure is a lot of stuff here." Sophisticated conversationalist, that's me. "What are you collecting?" Cady looked blank. The creep looked as if I'd asked him for directions to build a matter transmitter.

"All varieties of arts and crafts, multimedia, modern and traditional, also some ancient pieces."

"You're buying everything for resale?"

"Essentially, although some pieces I purchase on consignment for several museums."

My fingers were dying to uncover the nearest crate just to see if the rest of his collection matched his most recent acquisition. I started to move backward along the way we had come in. Wait a minute. Where was Charlie? He had been awfully quiet for the last couple of seconds. My head jerked around trying to locate him. Nothing. Suddenly the blackness got a whole lot deeper. The building sighed. Maybe it was just a draft, or then again maybe it was blood rushing past my eardrums. Shit, me and Cady alone. Charlie mysteriously disappeared. Cady's face was obscured by a feather's touch of light as if it were sprayed on a shimmering film. Hair I didn't know existed raised up along the northern ridge of my spine.

"Charlie," I called, backing my way blindly. Suppose this character collected more than mere artwork? What if he were their equivalent of specimen hunter? At the moment there was not the slightest shred of doubt that Cady was not human. He might very well be meaning to schedule our next meal for the outer side of Antares. Although nothing objective had changed except for Charlie's absence, that was more than sufficient to put all systems on red alert. Numero uno, get out of here. Feet do your duty. Fortunately feet were ahead of brain. I was running. So what if the stranger laughed. I had been in situations where survival depended on racing rather than reasoning. The next thing I knew my face connected with the floor and stars were pinwheeling in front of my eyes, matching the churning in my stomach. Cady's voice boomed.

"You really shouldn't run when you can't see where you're going. I was about to turn on the lights." At that, overhead lamps blinked into being. And Sheila and I were face to face. Wrapped in transparant material second cousin to Saran wrap, she was lying on a shelf along with other collector's items. She also appeared quite dead. Maybe she could be asleep with her eyes open? I immediately tossed that idea. The problem was that a living human is not covered with a stainless steel porcelain coating hard as a rock and just as cold to the touch.

They say the mind can deal with only one emotion at a time. Before I managed to struggle to my feet ignoring Cady's offer of assistance, fear had been replaced by a growing, burning sensation. My parents had a hell of a time raising me because of what they called my low flash point, which continued to be the bane of a professional and reasoned mature existence. At the moment it served me well. Time didn't exist. It was Cady's turn to retreat followed by a red haze.

"*Charlie!*" I screamed. If he was within hearing he'd come running. The next thing I was aware of was the feel of Cady's neck in my hands. All through this a little cube in the center of my brain was taking in data, analyzing and observing. In no way did it interfere with the raving beast in me.

"You M-F!" I shouted. I kept yelling more nastiness, spit, and bile. I was doing my best to strangle the bejesus out of him when Charlie dragged me off. Cady looked the worse for wear, but his finish hadn't been dented.

"I'm going to kill you," I shouted. "You creep"—going on in some detail to describe various means and distribution of parts of his body. Charlie was completely bewildered. I pointed. "See what he's done. That's Sheila. Dead. He murdered her."

"Please," said Cady, straightening his suit. "There has been a misunderstanding—a failure to communicate, as you call it."

"Kill him, Charlie." How easy to forget that Charlie didn't have a violent bone in his body. But Cady didn't know that.

"Your friend is not dead." He disentangled my hands from his lapels. Charlie, once he caught sight of the artist, couldn't take his eyes off her.

"Okay, okay, so what is she, posing in the nude?"

"If you will calm down . . . She is not dead, merely in a state of transformation. We offered her an opportunity to travel—to other worlds." If Cady had had real teeth they would have grated.

"As part of the cargo?" My voice rose.

"No, no, all living creatures are placed in a state of transformation. It's the nature of the translation effect."

"You won't get away with this." I started toward him again but Charlie's hold on my arm reasserted itself.

"It's at her own request!" Cady's glacial face was breaking down. He actually raised his voice.

"And mice lay goose-eggs."

Cady stopped breathing. For several heartbeats he was still, then he came back to himself.

"It has been decided that we want your cooperation. How would you like to talk to your friend and discover to your very own satisfaction that what I say is true?" He didn't wait for an answer. Smoothly he moved to Sheila and lifted her in his arms like a package of laundry. We followed Indian file through corridors lined with plastic, glass, wood- and metal-covered jars, bundles, crates, cans, suitcases, boxes, and jugs. I hungrily scanned the unbelievable numbers of tubes, spheres, and cylinders searching for anything that would help me understand what in the hell was going on here. Legitimate art collectors do not use old, unventilated warehouses for storage of valuables. Some of the contents were visible through transparent skins. Occasionally I caught a glimpse of something recognizable, like Brandice's plaster feet; once a Mardelaen wire sculpture flickered by.

Eventually we reached a suite of rooms in the rear. My anger had left an empty hole on its way out. Cady gently laid Sheila on a table. Charlie rushed in to help but Cady waved him away. He removed the sheathing from her head. Then he slid the table under the front of a complicated piece of equipment which took up most of the room. Thick cables disappeared up the back of the wall into holes in the ceiling. Twinkling patterns of pastel squares flickered into life as Cady touched the compact control board. He acted as if he knew what he was doing. Without twenty years of training I was in no position to understand. He swung one of the more familiar looking gadgets—like the head of a metallic grasshopper—over Sheila's body. More minute adjustments on grasshopper head, then he punched a "go" signal. The machine snicked, hummed, susurrated to itself. Hovering, touching, it moved slowly along the surface of her body. As it neared her feet, faint breathing began, then grew stronger. I leaned over. Sheila's eyes blinked. Consciousness sparkled. Tears ran down my cheeks as if I were a ten-year-old kid.

"Oh damn! Sheila, I thought you were dead." I hugged her. I didn't kiss her. She'll never be *that* lovable.

"What the hell is going on?" Sheila took in my face

and Cady, who was standing in the background along with Charlie.

"Your friend thought you were dead."

"Oh, darling, don't be so upset. Cady says he has some kind of suspended animation process. Unless he's sold me a bill of goods we're going to the stars." She raised her hands dramatically then took both my hands in hers. "Before we get too involved in explanations how about something to cover my body? I'm getting a chill and I'm giving you a thrill you don't deserve," she added, with a meaningful look at Charlie who had the grace to blush.

While we were getting settled to Sheila's satisfaction I asked, "When will you be back?"

"Don't know. Cady here says there will be a big demand for my style." She smirked.

"Then it's really goodby?" I was all choked up. That conceited bitch. My voice caught. Good Goddess. The thought overwhelmed me, millions of sentient beings subjected and/or exposed to Sheila's paintings. Auggh!

Is your coffee cold? Here, let me get you a warmup. Yeah, that's one of Sheila's pieces, done in her early period before she started mixing in the deeper purples.

How much is it? I couldn't accept anything less than $10,000. After all, you're dealing with an artist with an intergalactic reputation.

WILL ACADEME KILL SCIENCE FICTION?

by Jack Williamson

Tim Kirk - WITH APOLOGIES TO REMBRANDT VAN RIJN

A tall, easy-going, altogether friendly man, the writer is every bit the son of a rancher who moved his family to New Mexico by covered wagon. But his stories —ah!—for fifty years, Dr. Williamson has been the leading edge of the best of galaxy -and timespanning science fiction. He was a weather observer for the Army Air Corps in the South Pacific; his dissertation became the book, H. G. Wells: Critic of Progress, *and he taught SF at the University of Eastern New Mexico from 1964 until his retirement—from teaching, not from writing—last year.*

We science-fictioneers lie stretched on a cold stone slab. The hooded academicians are slicing into us with their critical scalpels, lecturing their students on our secret inner workings and debating the function and value of this organ or that, as if we were already dead.

I don't think we are—not just yet. But a lot of us can't help wondering just how much good this scholarly dissection is going to do us. It's a new and sudden thing, all the consequences not yet clear.

Already, however, the teachers of science fiction are probably earning more out of it than the writers do. Though criticism is seldom directly paid, under the "publish or perish" laws of academic survival it's the path toward tenure and promotion. The criticism of SF has tapped rich new veins for researchers, and I can think of writers who seem to be trying harder to impress the critics than to please their readers. I'm afraid the critical tail has begun to wag the creative dog.

Personally, as writer and teacher and occasional critic, I have been in several camps. Retired from teaching now, I'm once more a full-time writer—fiction turns out to be more fun than criticism. Here, I want to try an objective survey of the benefits and hazards of this somewhat surprising academic recognition. I hope these comments will interest readers and maybe be useful to teachers.

§ § §

When I began writing, back in the 1920s, SF still had no familiar name. Hugo Gernsback was still calling it "scientification," a term that baffled most people—I used to tell my friends that I was writing adventure stories with a science background. With no book publishers interested—certainly no scholarly critics—it was restricted to a few such pulps as Gernsback's *Amazing Stories* and the old, all-fiction *Argosy*.

Though the SF pulps multiplied during the 1930s, we had little notice anywhere else until after World

War II, when a few fans set up such small firms as Fantasy Press and Gnome Press to begin reprinting their favorite magazine serials in hard covers. Their success brought major publishers into the field, with the movies and TV soon to follow.

I think most fans catch the virus young. The early pulps carried pages of fan letters in microscopic print, most of them written by such enthusiastic kids as I was. No doubt most got over the mania, but some of us didn't.

The typical critic—like the typical writer and the typical SF teacher—is, I believe, one of those young fans who attained age and education without losing interest. Examples are such grown-up fans as Damon Knight and Tom Clareson and the late Jim Blish.

In the late 1950s a few of these fans-turned-academics, finding themselves together in the great Modern Language Association, set up a science fiction seminar. This led in time to the SFRA, the Science Fiction Research Association, which now has several hundred members.

The newsletter of the seminar has evolved into *Extrapolation,* the original scholarly fanzine. Others are listed below, among other aids for the SF teacher. In addition to these, there has been a great deal of informed comment in some of the non-academic fanzines. The first thin trickle of critical books is swelling into a flood. Taplinger, for example, is issuing a "Twenty-First Century Authors Series," the first six volumes to be about Asimov, Clarke, Heinlein, Bradbury, Dick, and Le Guin; golden ground for ambitious academics!

Though I can remember when librarians were scornfully excluding such illiterate trash as Edgar Rice Burroughs and *Astounding Stories*, a decade or two ago they suddenly began to prize it, collecting books and long runs of the brittle old pulps and the working papers of every available SF writer from Ackerman to Zelazny. Hundreds of rare old titles are being reprinted now in high-priced library editions by Gregg Press and Garland and others.

§ § §

The academic boom began with the course taught by Mark Hillegas at Colgate in 1962—Sam Moskowitz and others had conducted special lecture courses earlier. I used a news story about Mark's course to get approval for one of my own at Eastern New Mexico University, which I taught for a dozen years.

In the past decade they have multiplied wonderfully. Gathering facts in 1969 for a talk on "SF in the University," I learned of some two dozen courses. The talk led to a little publication of my own, *Teaching SF,* which was a descriptive listing intended to help convince the academic skeptics that SF had really become a legitimate subject. By 1974, when I decided to give up the project because it was getting out of bounds, I had collected descriptions of some 500 courses offered at the college level in the United States and Canada.

By that time, SF had swept on into the high schools, becoming a remarkably popular elective. A chance mention in *English Journal* brought orders for hundreds of copies of *Teaching SF.* That booklet is now out of date and out of print, but there must be several thousand high school courses, some of them in multiple sections with hundreds of students enrolled.

The courses are hard to describe because they differ so much. Most of them, I think, might be placed somewhere along a broad spectrum that ranges from futurology to fantasy. At the futurological extreme, the emphasis is on technological and sociological extrapolations in the real world; at the opposite extreme, the emphasis is on symbolic myth or "transcendence" or stylistic value or pure escape.

Most of the successful teachers are motivated, I think, by a sense that SF has a special relevance to life in our transitional times. In a world of disturbing change, it can become folklore or gospel. Hard science fiction, such as Wells's *When the Sleeper Wakes,* probes alternative futures by means of reasoned extrapolation from the known present in much the same way that good historical fiction reconstructs the probable past. Even far-out fantasy can present significant human values. Deriving its most cogent ideas from the tensions between permanence and change, SF combines the diversions of novelty with its own realistic faithfulness to the fact of change.

More than half the college courses are listed in English, but others have been offered in a score of departments ranging from astronomy and physics through the social sciences to philosophy and religion. The high school courses and a few in the lower grades are commonly taught as literature but are sometimes used to motivate reluctant readers and awaken interests generally.

Though I suppose the great majority has not yet been touched by SF, hundreds of thousands or millions of students have already been turned on—by fan friends, by juvenile novels, by *Star Trek* and *2001* and now by *Star Wars*. The alert teacher can capture their attention, simply by sharing their interest.

SF still appeals to the young, as always, because so much of it is set in the futures in which they will be living. Though the details of new inventions and alien invaders may seem fantastic, the TV kiddie shows on Saturday morning have already introduced them—SF can't be as new to anybody now as once it was for me!—and accelerating change has become almost the first fact of life.

§ § §

There is no standard syllabus for the SF course at any level. Though hundreds of teachers have been inquiring, I'm not sure we need it. One joy of the course, as things stand now, is the freedom it offers the instructor to select the writers that excite him and to communicate his own excitement.

When I began my own course, there were no special texts. I used the low-priced mass paperbacks—still low-priced then!—from such houses as Ace and Avon and Ballantine and Berkley and Bantam and DAW. They are still bargains. Issued for newsstand sale, however, they tend to drop out of print before college bookstores can stock them.

Though scholars have been trying to select a canon, the lists of books in use still vary vastly. Tabulating nearly 80 reading lists a few years ago, I found some 300 titles named, half of them only once. Even the most popular titles were used in no more than a third of the classes. That was before the special texts were numerous, and before the mass publishers began increasing their efforts to reach the schools, but the results may still be useful.

The dozen most popular titles were Asimov's *I, Robot,* Bradbury's *The Martian Chronicles*, Heinlein's *The Moon Is a Harsh Mistress* and *Stranger in a Strange Land,* Herbert's *Dune,* Huxley's *Brave New World,* Le Guin's *Left Hand of Darkness,* Miller's *Canticle for Leibowitz*, Pohl and Kornbluth's *Space Merchants,* Silverberg's *Science Fiction Hall of Fame,* Vol. I, and Wells's *Time Machine* and *War of the Worlds.*

Ingenious teachers have brought life to their classes with all sorts of challenging projects, such as designing new worlds and creatures to fit them. Good audiovisual aids are now available, some described below. Such classic SF films as *Metropolis* can be rented for nominal fees. SF writers can be invited to visit the classroom—a few command high lecture fees, but many are pleased to meet new readers anywhere. (There is a speakers bureau as part of the Science Fiction Writers of America; the address is listed at the end of this article.)

§ § §

Though no course is typical, I suppose my own is a reasonable random sample. Offered at the junior level in college, it generally drew more people than I really wanted for the mixed lecture-and-discussion approach. A few were veteran fans, a few more wanted to write, most were simply curious about science fiction or looking for three upper-division hours in English.

Working toward a general appreciation of SF, we considered definitions and origins; history and types; writing techniques and markets; the uses of SF for entertainment, prediction, and social comment; standards and literary values.

(Science fiction, as I like to define it, is fiction based on the imagined exploration of scientific possibility. The distinction from fantasy—or from other sorts of fantasy—lies in the word *possibility*. In a different way than SF, fantasy asks for Coleridge's famous poetic faith resulting from a willing suspension of disbelief in the impossible.

(This sense of possiblity is of course only a small part of the effect of any individual story. Once embarked on the narrative flow, the reader is caught and carried on by the old appeals of mood and style and theme, drawn by the drama of characters in conflict. But still, I think, he wants the assumption that just maybe, somewhere, somehow, it really could happen. Any crude violation of accepted science can break the spell.)

The history of SF can begin nearly anywhere, even with the prehistoric Greeks. If we look at it as a response to technological change, however, it is only in the last couple of centuries that this has been apparent. Brian Aldiss makes a good case for Mary Shelley's *Frankenstein,* published in 1818, as the starting point.

Poe wrote SF not much later, in the same Gothic tradition. He influenced Jules Verne, whose lively tales of new inventions and far adventure earned world acclaim. H. G. Wells, however, was the real founding father of modern SF. A student under T. H. Huxley, he had learned evolution and become our first futurologist, gaining an understanding of our nature and our niche in an uncaring cosmos that Poe and Verne had lacked.

Scholars and anthologists have classified SF in all sorts of ways. Asimov, for example, once called it primitive (1818–1926), adventure (1926–1938), gadget (1938–1945), and social science fiction (1945 to the present)—the only sort worth critical attention. This scheme does fit the American SF magazines, but I can quite agree that Wells was primitive.

A more meaningful distinction, I believe, certainly one more rewarding in the classroom, is the division between the utopians and the dystopians, between the optimists and pessimists about man's place in the universe and his chances of using reason and science to build a better future.

This issue is probably older than the art of lighting fire, but it is now more urgent every day, as the whole world must somehow balance all the increasing expectations of growing populations against the limits of our resources and the dangers of environmental damage.

Swift foresaw this war, and the Luddites were early skirmishers. Sir Charles Snow described it 20 years ago, in his defense of the culture of science against the traditional literary academics. New battles are raging now over every pipeline, every strip mine, every nuclear reactor. The conflict is clearly coming toward some kind of climax, the outcome not yet sure. We're all involved. The issue has been a central theme of SF, at least since Wells, and students are likely to be delighted with fiction that expresses their own concerns.

Class readings on the dystopian side can begin with the last two books of *Gulliver*—Swift is satirizing the pioneer scientists in the Royal Society. I think Wells, especially in *The Island of Dr. Moreau* and *The First Men in the Moon,* is writing more voyages for Gulliver. Zamyatin's *We* echoes Wells; Aldous Huxley and George Orwell echo both. This dystopian line comes on down through my own *Hu-*

manoids, through Fred Pohl and the New Wave, to Harlan Ellison and other.

The utopians are seldom quite so effective—I think the dystopians have an accidental advantage in the tragic drama inherent in their doomsdays. But there is faith in man's reason and hope for his future in the *Odyssey,* in Plato's *Republic*, in Lord Bacon, in Heinlein's juvenile explorers of the universe and Asimov's positronic robots and Clarke's visions of human evolution from caveman to spaceman.

A writer myself, I probably gave more classroom attention to technique than most teachers would. We discussed problems of plot and character and theme and style and viewpoint, sometimes using a little paperback of my own, *People Machines.* Students did two assignments each semester, either critical or creative.

Most of them wrote stories—or sometimes turned in a poem, a chapter of a novel, an original painting, a cartoon strip, a recorded SF drama, a futuristic costume—any of which I cheerfully accepted. Few of the stories reached the professional level, but they were nearly always interesting, the writing often remarkably better than that in the ordinary term paper.

The whole class shared in reading and evaluation, and we read outstanding items aloud. Now and then, when students volunteered to be editors, we produced a class magazine; and a good many of our productions reached the school's literary magazine—which I was sponsoring—to win awards there.

For students who were interested, we discussed the worlds of fandom and writing as a career, passing around a variety of fanzines, prozines, original anthologies, criticism, and the new SF picture books. A few students have reported sales, and at least one has an accepted novel in progress—student writers are sometimes highly gifted, but—fortunately for us professionals—they are very seldom obsessed enough with success to make the sort of sustained effort that it took for even such able people as Bradbury and Ellison to break into the game.

Considering the uses of science fiction, I think it must first of all offer entertainment, before the futurology or the social comment can matter. For most readers, entertainment means escape. Though a few young writers are scornful of that, creating good escape fiction is a high and admirable art. Even when the writer aims at something more, entertainment is basic. The bored reader is lost.

Here, I suspect, the critics are becoming a threat. Praising obscure symbolism, far-out experiments in style, and adherence to party dogma, they are too often able to persuade a talented writer to neglect essential story values. (In my own uninvited opinion, Chip Delany has sometimes been among the victims.)

In a limited but significant way, SF is predictive—predicting nearly everything, we're sometimes right! The limits are narrow. As Wells discovered with *When the Sleeper Wakes,* futurology and fiction mix rather poorly. The writer in search of originality and story drama often does well to select the less likely future.

Yet, as everybody knows, we did foresee space flight and atomic bombs and organ transplants. That's a key item in our popular image and a chief reason for the growing popularity of science fiction. In our age of runaway technological change, future shock is real and common. I think SF can be our best defense, allowing us to learn to ride tomorrow's waves before they break over us.

Much SF is social comment—in a sense, perhaps it all is, being produced by present-day writers for present-day readers, its imagined futures all drawn from present-day concerns. Mainstream critics tend to see no other use. Kingsley Amis, for example, considered SF as social satire and not much else in *New Maps of Hell.*

On literary value, we must appeal to Ted Sturgeon's Law: Nine-tenths of anything is crap. The other tenth of SF is, I think, comparable in lasting worth and interest to the best tenth of any body of work being done today. Witness the widening international recognition of such writers as Phil Dick and Ursula Le Guin and Stanislaw Lem.

Yet, despite all we claim for it, SF is still widely suspect, still fatally stained from its pulp past. In the publishing industry, it's merely another category, like mystery or western or Gothic. If the SF label on a recognizable package can assure moderate sales, it seems also to prevent large sales. Winning best-seller status, such writers as Vonnegut deny the label.

A few people have decided that SF should stand for something else—speculative fiction or speculative fantasy or speculative fabulations. I think they're mistaken. I'm afraid the climb up the giddy spires of Literary Art has taken them too far from any solid base in scientific believability and human interest.

To a limited extent, as others have suggested, SF may be merging into the mainstream. Certainly, as it grows in popularity, more and more mainstream writers are attracted to it. Often, however, they show little understanding of either the methods of science or the tested conventions of SF. Or perhaps my old prejudices are showing.

In any case, there's room for everybody. The SF audience has many appetites. Burroughs' tales of Barsoom are still in wide demand, along with Vonnegut's satire and Phil Dick's probing of apparent realities and Chip Delany's *Dhalgren*.

§ § §

Getting back at last to our initial question: *Will academe kill SF?* I don't think so. The effects of our late welcome into the ivory tower will probably be mixed, but SF is a sturdy young giant with a history of survival. The New Wave is a case in point. Greeted with cries of alarm, it has receded to leave the whole field richer in technique and awareness.

I do suspect that the critics are luring a few promising writers into the formless indulgence and the willful obscurity that has destroyed the popularity of modern poetry. I must admit, too, that many of the new teachers are not at home with SF—their desperate appeals for help are proof of that.

Ben Bova and Jim Gunn have debated the teaching of SF, in *Analog* editorials. Both are respected experts, Ben as editor and writer, Jim as writer, critic, and teacher of an outstanding SF course at the University of Kansas. Ben, still smarting under the way the TV industry mauled and cheapened Harlan Ellison's fine original concept for *Starlost*, was afraid that poorly qualified teachers would do the same sort of thing in the classroom, turning students off. Jim, speaking from his college experience, is convinced that good SF, in spite of untrained teachers, will turn them on.

I think Jim is right. In our TV world, many students don't arrive as serious readers. Leading them to appreciate Shakespeare or Joyce or Dostoevsky is always difficult, often impossible. I have found it far easier to involve them in SF, perhaps because its futures have come to seem more real and challenging than the past.

§ § §

In the high schools alone, hundreds of thousands of kids are being exposed each year to classic SF. Some few teachers, I suppose, limit them to the dated works of Hawthorne and Poe, or take them on searches for symbols and themes the writers never intended, or bog them down in dry research assignments, but many another teacher is as creative and enthusiastic as our arthritic educational establishment allows. Many a bright student, no matter where he first meets SF, will recognize it as an exciting and essential new language, invented to make better sense of our fast-evolving world.

For the teacher at any level who understands and cares about SF, the course is a rare opportunity. There are aids waiting, some outlined below. Though paths enough have been explored, there is freedom left to select your own direction, toward a broad humanism or toward nearly any special field. Most of the students will be above average; a few will be fans, already full of the writers they admire. For all, there is enjoyment and intellectual liberation in science fiction. Far from killing it, academe promises to enrich it with new readers, new writers, and new dimensions of interest.

RESOURCES FOR THE SF TEACHER

Periodicals:

Besides the small handful of such professional magazines as *IA'sfm*, there are at any time several hundred fanzines, dozens worth reading. Labors of love, they appear unannounced and vanish untraced. They have printed some of the best SF criticism, and some of the worst, all of it hard to locate now. Here are a few important and stable titles:

Locus. Edited by Charles N. Brown, 34 Ridgewood Lane, Oakland Ca. 94611. (12 issues, $9.00) The indispensable SF news magazine.

Extrapolation. Edited by Thomas D. Clareson, Box 3186, The College of Wooster, Wooster OH 44691. "The Journal of the MLA Seminar on Science Fiction, also serving the Science Fiction Research Association." (2 issues yearly, $4.00) The oldest of the academic fanzines.

Science Fiction Studies. Edited by R. D. Mullen and Darko Suvin, Department of English, Indiana State University, Terre Haute, IN 47809. (3 issues, $6.00) Seriously academic and often useful, but sometimes too pedantic and doctrinaire for my taste.

Foundation. Edited by Peter Nicholls, North East London Polytechnic, Longbridge Road, Essex, RM8 2AS, England. Brighter and more relaxed than most academic journals.

Delap's F&SF Review. Edited by Richard Delap, 1226 North Laurel Ave., W. Hollywood CA 90046. (12 issues, $13.50; libraries, $18.00) Full and knowledgeable reviews of SF in all forms, essential for librarians, recommended for the teacher and the serious reader.

Algol. Edited by Andrew Porter, PO Box 4175, New York NY 10017. Non-academic, but handsome, informed, and readable.

Science Fiction Review. Edited by Richard E. Geis, PO Box 11408, Portland OR 97211. Highly personal comment by an intelligent and articulate critic.

Audiovisual Aids:

James Gunn has produced a series of filmed lectures on SF by writers and editors in the field, available for rental or purchase from the Audio-Visual Center, the University of Kansas, Lawrence KS 66045. Especially recommended are those by Asimov and Pohl, and the one by Ackerman on SF films.

Science Fiction: Jules Verne to Ray Bradbury is a slide-cassette program (3 cassettes and 240 slides) issued by the Center for the Humanities, Inc., 2 Holland Ave., White Plains NY 10603. ($169.50) A basic introduction, which I like.

For visiting science fiction lecturers, write to the Science Fiction Writers Speakers Bureau, care of Mildred Downey Broxon, 2207 Fairview Avenue East, Seattle, WA 98102. Send a stamped, self-addressed envelope for a descriptive brochure.

Handbooks for Teachers

Calkins, Elizabeth, and Barry McGhan. *Teaching Tomorrow: A Handbook of Science Fiction for Teachers.* Pflaum/Standard, 1972. Brief paperback for high school teachers.

Friend, Beverly. *Science Fiction: The Classroom in Orbit.* Educational Impact, 1974. Short paperback for both high school and college teachers.

Williamson, Jack, ed. *Science Fiction: Education for Tomorrow.* Mirage Press, PO Box 7687, Baltimore MD 21207. (Delayed, due in early 1978.) A comprehensive teaching guide in three sections, "The Topic," "The Teachers," "The Tools." Articles by Asimov, Bova, Gunn, Le Guin, Pohl, and 20-odd others. Introduction by Carl Sagan.

Criticism and History:

Aldiss, Brian. *Billion Year Spree.* Doubleday, 1973. An outstanding critical history to about 1950, rather superficial on period since.

______. *Science Fiction Art.* Bounty Books (Crown Publishers), 1975. A stunning picture book with intelligent text.

Barron, Neil. *Anatomy of Wonder: Science Fiction.* Bowker, 1976. Recent, scholarly, and comprehensive. Lengthy annotated bibliography, essential for librarians and collectors.

Bretnor, Reginald, ed. *The Craft of Science Fiction.* Harper & Row, 1975. The best text on writing SF.

______. *Science Fiction, Today and Tomorrow.* Harper & Row, 1974. (Also in Penguin paperback) A broad and useful survey by some 15 writers.

Clareson, Thomas D. *Science Fiction Criticism: An Annotated Checklist.* Kent State U. Press, 1972. Useful listing, 800 items.

Gunn, James E. *Alternate Worlds.* Prentice Hall, 1975. (Also in paperback) A fine critical history with hundreds of photographs.

Hillegas, Mark Robert. *The Future as Nightmare: H. G. Wells and the Anti-Utopians.* Oxford, 1967. An outstanding study of Wells and his pessimistic followers.

Johnson, William, ed. *Focus on the Science Fiction Film.* Prentice-Hall, 1972. Recommended.

Williamson, Jack. *H. G. Wells: Critic of Progress.* Mirage, 1973. On the futurology and the great early SF of Wells.

Wollheim, Donald A. *The Universe Makers.* Harper & Row, 1971. Personal comment by an influential editor and publisher.

Classroom Texts;

Scarce at first, special SF texts are now too numerous to list in full. Since they are expensive, many instructors will prefer to use the lower-priced books from the mass publishers, which have become easier for schools to obtain. Here are typical titles:

Allen David. *Science Fiction: An Introduction.* Cliff Notes, 1973. Includes useful essays on a dozen important SF novels.

Allen, Richard Stanley, ed. *Science Fiction: The Future.* Harcourt, 1971. An excellent anthology; futurological emphasis.

Bova, Ben, ed. *Science Fiction Hall of Fame,* Vols. IIA & IIB. Doubleday, 1973. (Also in Avon paperback—a bargain!) Classic SF novelettes to 1965.

Katz, Harvey A., Patricia Warrick, and Martin Harry Greenberg, eds. *Introductory Psychology through Science Fiction.* Rand McNally, 1974. Typical of numerous collections by these and other editors, using SF to introduce nearly everything.

Sargent, Pamela, ed. *Women of Wonder: Science Fiction Stories by Women about Women.* Vintage, 1975. An excellent collection; outstanding introductory essay.

Scholes, Robert, and Eric S. Rabkin. *Science Fiction: History, Science, Vision.* Oxford, 1977. (Paper, $2.95) A thorough and excellent recent text. Recommended.

Silverberg, Robert, ed. *The Mirror of Infinity: A Critics' Anthology of Science Fiction.* Harper & Row, 1970. (Also in paperback) Well-chosen stories, each with a foreword by a different critic, making the book a useful historical survey of SF from Wells to the seventies.

———. *Science Fiction Hall of Fame,* Vol. I. Doubleday, 1971. (Also in Avon paperback—another bargain!) Classic short stories to 1965, selected by members of the SFWA.

Spinrad, Norman. *Modern Science Fiction.* Doubleday (Anchor paperback), 1974. Good historical anthology with essays defending the New Wave.
Wells, H. G. *The Time Machine / The War of the Worlds; A Critical Edition,* ed. Frank D. McConnell. Oxford, 1977. (Paper, $4.00) Wells's two most popular SF novels, with well-chosen critical essays.
Wilson, Robin Scott. *Those Who Can: A Science Fiction Reader.* Mentor, 1973. Twelve writers accompany their reprinted short stories with essays on plot, character, setting, theme, point of view, and style.

A SOLUTION TO THE THIRD DR. MOREAU (from page 38)

The question is easily solved by time-reversing the event. If the container was filled after 50 hours, it was 1/7 filled after 49 hours.

That should have been easy. But consider, now, a more difficult question. Suppose Dr. Moreau III had put *seven* microbes into the container instead of one. After how many hours would the container have been 1/7 full of microbes? See page 153 for the answer.

HEAL THE SICK, RAISE THE DEAD

by Jesse Peel

Mr. Peel tells us that he is 29, married, with two children. During his yearning-to-be-a-writer-someday-when-I-have-time period, he has been a lifeguard, a swimming teacher, an aluminum-salesman-and-fork-lift-operator, a private investigator, a kung-fu instructor, and a male nurse. Currently, he's working at a family medical clinic as a Physician's Assistant—sort of half-nurse, half-doctor, half-technician, and general flunky. The writer lives with his family in the bayous of Louisiana; this story is his first sale.

After I finished attaching the last of the electrodes to the body, I looked at the girl, making it into a question with my raised eyebrows. She nodded, her thin-and-young face very pale. I turned back to my instruments—all the connections seemed to be correct—so I punched the power switch. The body gave a small, convulsive twitch; there was the smell of burned hair, then . . . nothing.

"Sometimes it takes a while," I said. Anything important usually does. I thought about my own decision. Soon, I'd likely be lying on a table like the one I now stood next to.

She nodded again, and I wanted to tell her that in this case, it might take longer than a while—it might well take forever.

Despite the cryo-table and the holding-embalm, six days was a long time, a hell of a long time. I didn't know of any case ever brought back over a week or eight days, and anything over five days was usually good enough to make the medical journals.

The girl stood by the body, her slight frame tense and trembling. Her fingers were knitted together, the knuckles white and bloodless. Small beads of sweat stood out on her upper lip and neck, despite the hard chill of the crematorium. Her eyes never left the inert form of the dead boy.

I mostly watched my instruments, lost in my own thoughts. It was cold, and I always got cramps from standing too long when it was cold. I moved about, shifting from one leg to the other, to keep the circulation going. The smell of burnt hair was rivaled by that of stale death; there were over a thousand bodies lying on tables around us.

There was nothing yet to see on the scopes. The ECG was flat, the ECG straight-lined. Total Systems Output was nil, and enzymes were dormant. The polyvital injection/infusion was running well, despite the collapsed state of the blood vessels but six days were still six days.

I glanced at the lifeless body, and tried to see myself there. I couldn't picture it, being dead. I wondered again how much that had to do with the whole business.

§ § §

I'd figured her for a grafter this morning when she first came in. But the spiderweb skintight she wore was revealing enough to show that she had no obvious scars from prior surgery. No matter how good a medic is, there is always something—a discoloration here, a stretchmark there. She was clean, like a baby.

She had high, small breasts and a thin, leggy body. Her feet were covered with clear spray-on slippers. There was an odor of some musky perfume about her that was pleasant enough, and I figured that she was maybe fifteen.

No graft marks, so today might be her first time. The latest was to have the little finger of the right hand replaced with a live coral snake. Deadly, but who cared? It was novel—this month. Last big fad had everyone wearing raccoon tails for crotch cover. Next month, who could tell?

"What can I do for you?" I asked, giving her my best professional medic smile. I wondered if I had any snakes left in the cryo-tank—business had been good this month.

"I want a Reconstruct," she blurted, her voice a high quaver.

Reconstruct? Damn! So much for my *augenblick* diagnosis of neophyte grafter! I tried to hide my surprise with a question. "How old are you?"

She hesitated for a second. "Thirteen—almost fourteen!"

Missed again. I'd thought fifteen generous, but thirteen? That was much too young to be asking for a Reconstruct. Legally, anyway. Not that too many people paid a hell of a lot of attention to the laws these days.

"Who's this package you want defrosted? Parent?"

She shook her head, and looked down at the floor.

"Sibling?"

She brought her eyes up to meet mine. "Pronger," she said softly.

Well. She didn't look thirteen, and I supposed that if they were big enough, they were old enough. I looked at her small-and-slim body, and sighed. They were maturing earlier all the time, those that were left. When I was young, they'd have put you under the jail and left you there for sleeping with a girl that age. Except that a mob would probably have dragged you out and hanged you from the nearest tree in short order.

I sighed again. When I was young. That was so long ago, it seemed like a million years.

Maybe I was getting senile, living in the past, I thought. Sure, senile at fifty-four.

That was young, fifty-four. If you wanted to bother, you could figure on three times that age before you died, given the state of modern medicine. If you wanted to bother. Hardly anybody did, I mean, what for? I am one of the oldest people I know—maybe one of the oldest period.

I pulled myself back to the girl. "When did he terminate?"

"Last Friday."

Today was Thursday. That irritated me! Damn people who held off until the last minute! What did they expect, miracles? "Waited kind of long, didn't you?"

"I was . . . afraid." It was a whimper, a plea.

Go on, I scolded myself, make the little girl cry.

"How old was he?"

"Fourteen."

Another child. "How'd he die? Accident?"

She took a deep breath, and said it with a rush. "Self'struct!"

God Damn! Tired of life at that tender age! Suddenly I felt very old and tired and alone. I looked quickly down at my desk, visualizing the plastic bottle of capsules there. I was nearly four times his age, I had that kind of right—but God, a fourteen year-old boy?

§ § §

On my scopes, I was finally getting some activity. A small spiking on the EEG, not much, but something, at least.

I increased the power input slightly. Easy does it, I told myself, don't fry him. I was curious to hear his version, provided I could land him, and it would be good work. Good work was something to be proud of, something else people rarely bothered with any more.

He had been a handsome kid when he was alive. Some medic had done a rotten job on a pair of matched leopard-fur shoulder caplets. They were the only transplants he'd been wearing when he'd died. A few scars were scattered over his body, remnants of past surgeries, but not all that many. Pretty conservative, for a teener.

I looked around the crematorium, noticing how nearly full it was. Looked like they'd have to run the ovens in a day or two, to clear the tables for the next batch. I could taste the bitter dregs of the holding-embalm left in the air by the air'ditioners, and I felt the cold worse because of the clammy dead, I fancied. I spotted only two guards roaming about, but I knew that there were others. There were certain . . . people in our society who had all sorts of uses for fresh bodies.

Another blip on my scopes—some ventricular fib on the ECG. The heart was tough, even after death. I began to think that I might get this boy moving after all. The timer said twenty minutes had passed, and that wasn't good, but there was still a chance out to half an hour.

But five more minutes passed without any change. Then seven. Eight. Crap, the organs must be too far gone. Sorry, kid, I thought, as I reached for the power switch.

Just then, the body turned its head. The girl squealed and I turned up the strength on the booster-relay. I had gross muscle!

Three more minutes passed and then the fibrillation converted. Damned if I didn't get a spotty but definite sinus rhythm! A block, sure, but it was pumping! If autonomics were still workable, that meant some fine control was possible. Maybe even speech.

The EEG had steeled down to only a mild epileptogenic focus, so I fed the neural circuits more juice. Oxy-lack damage was difficult to overcome, but the polyvital could soothe a great deal of brain damage and rot—temporarily.

Now or never, I thought. I kicked in the bellows pump, and the lungs started to inflate. If they held. . . .

"Uuunnhhh." A windy moan, the voice of the dead.

"Roj? Oh, Roj! I'm here!"

His eyes opened. They were cloudy, of course, and blind. Optic nerves were always the first to go—very few Reconstructs were sighted, even those only a day or two gone. But the eighth cranial, the auditory, hung on for some reason. It was always the last to leave, so it was likely that he'd be able to hear.

". .Te. .Tefi?" Ah, some vocal cords. It was that eerie drone of speech I had heard so many times before. Mostly wind, rushing through a voice-box that had lost much of its elasticity. There was little tongue or lip involved.

"Oh, Roj!" she cried, reaching out to touch him.

"Don't!" I yelled, my voice an echo in the vast room. "You'll short him out!" She jerked her hand back, and I relaxed a little. Likely short yourself out too, I thought. Besides, you wouldn't like the feel of his flesh. It would be like a just-thawed steak.

". .efi?. . .wh. .why...didn' . .youuu..uuhhh...you..... uuhhh. . ."

The girl started to cry. "I'm sorry," she whispered with a sob. I watched as a tear fell onto the cryo-table. It spattered, and froze into a thousand smaller tears.

"After you, I mean, I was scared, after you were. . . ."

" 's okay. . .swee'.....efi. . . . .uuhhh.....'s.....like they ssaid. . . ."

The dead boy struggled, fighting against the bellows pump which restricted his speech. He fought for air which had no other use to him now except to run his decaying vocal cords.

"..onderful..here.. .like they ssaid...'eaceful. 'alm...sso.nice." Another pause, waiting for the air. "...friendss...here...all of the...but..youuu... ."

She started to sob, her body shaking. The knobs of my instruments felt suddenly hard and lifeless in my hands. Even after all this time, I could still feel the sadness. Even after all the people I'd brought back.

A self'struct pact. Only she couldn't go through with it at the end. So she had brought him back. For what? To say she was sorry? Could that matter to him? Or to find out if it were really true, what they said about the Other Side? To hear it from one she knew and could trust, to know that Life After Death existed, after all.

But did she know? The boy's story was familiar. It was like, but unlike many others I had heard. It was good to hear it, since I had almost decided. It helped to push my fears into the distance. It helped.

But looking at the girl's face, I wasn't happy. She was getting the same message, more, it was her dead lover saying it. No, I thought, not you. Me, certainly, but not you, not at your age. Don't listen. Wait—thirty, or forty years, a hundred years, then decide. But not now!

I jerked my eyes down, to see the digitals dropping. He was fading. It had taken every bit of my skill, along with a great deal of luck to pull him in, and now I was losing him. But I tried, for her sake—and my own. I punched in full power. The smell of burning hair grew stronger. The body shook, but it was no good. He was gone, this time, forever.

Once, we healed the sick. Now, we raised the dead. I was as bad as all the rest, I did it too. That ability, that power of god-like strength, that curse was going to be the death of mankind. I looked at the girl, and I knew.

"I'm sorry," I said, not just meaning the loss of the boy.

"Don't be," she said, smiling through the tears. "It's all right now."

But I knew that it wasn't all right. Not now, not ever. She had made up her mind, but it wasn't all right. It was wrong, and it was as much my fault as any man's.

I repacked my instruments. Even after thirty years as a medic, I still hated to lose a patient, regardless that he was already dead. All I wanted to do now was get out, into the city-stale but alive air.

Inside my ancient and much-repaired hovercraft, we sat quietly for a minute, letting the autoglide fly us back to my office. I knew what she was thinking, but it was wrong.

Why?, shouted a voice inside my head. Weren't you thinking the same thing?

That's different, I argued with myself. I am older. I—

Hah!, said the voice.

"So you are going to do it," I said. It was not a question.

She nodded, smiling and unafraid now.

"You can't! You're only a child!" I exploded.

"Roj is waiting for me!"

"There are a thousand boys—"

"No! They are not Roj!"

"But to kill yourself—"

"So what? Here is only here! There is perfect! It's like everybody said, you heard him!"

Yes, I'd heard him. Him, and all the others. Still, I had to try.

"You don't know what life has to offer!"

"I do so! I'm not a baby! I've been places, done things! Why go through it all over again? Why does it even matter? Roj is *there,* waiting for me!"

"But—"

"You heard him!" She threw herself back deeply

into the hovercraft's worn seat, her arms crossed to shut me out.

How could I argue with it? How could I fight a voice from the lips of her own dead lover? Who would not be taken in, convinced totally by the words of a father, mother, or a sister—or a wife?

I stared through the pitted plastic window at the city beneath us. Mostly deserted now, a far cry from the days before the Reconstruct process. Maybe if Mali had lived, had made it until the process had been perfected. . . . No. It was long past, and I'd never hear it from my own wife.

I turned back to the girl. "Listen," I said, feeling desperate. For some reason, it was important that she know, that she understand. I caught her shoulders, feeling her smooth skin and firm muscle under my hands.

"When the Reconstruct concept was first created, there were a lot of theories. One of the most important was thrown out, because nobody wanted to believe it. That theory says that what the dead say is not real!"

She shook her head and struggled, but I wouldn't let her go.

"It says that the human brain refuses to accept its own death, so it makes up a story, to convince itself that it will not die! That what the dead say when you bring them back is only that story, played back a final time, like a recording! That's why the stories are different, because they are subjective, not because there are really different realities on the Other Side!"

She stared at me, not wanting to hear it.

"Don't you understand? It could all be a lie! You could be killing yourself for nothing!" There. I'd said it. But who was I really trying to convince?

"You heard, you heard!" She screamed, starting to cry. "Roj said, he said, he said—"

I let her go, and slumped back into my own seat. Yes. Roj had said.

§ § §

The girl was gone, and I sat alone at my desk, staring at the drawer. Had I convinced her? Planted a seed of the smallest doubt? I didn't know. Probably not, but maybe. Somebody had to convince them, the young ones. What if the theory was valid?

What even, if the theory was wrong? Suppose there was Life After Death—what then? Why would there be any point in staying alive. Or what point in being born in the first place? It was a question that had been debated by the best minds we had, and no answer had been found.

At least, not in this life. There was one way for anyone who wished to find out. I took the bottle of capsules from the drawer, and shook them about inside their plastic prison. I was older than most, surely I had the right to do as I wished. I had heard all the stories: It was Heaven, Valhalla, Nirvana, Paradise. Nobody ever said that it was Hell—at worst, it was a much better place than here.

But if I did it, who would be left to try and keep the young ones going? And what if it were a lie? What if the whole thing was a massive con game, a trick of the human mind on itself, who would be around to try and keep the human race going?

I was supposed to be a healer, a life-giver, a medic. It was my job, wasn't it? But I was tired, and how much could one man be expected to do?

I poured the blue-and-green capsules out onto the desk, touching the slick-and-light one-way tickets to where? Heaven, or oblivion? I stirred them around with my finger, hearing the tiny sound they made on my plastic desk. I was almost sure, until I had met the girl today, and brought back her dead lover.

Was this the way the world was to end, not with a bang or a whimper, but with an expectant smile?

Could all those people be wrong? There was only one way I could be sure, only one way. Carefully, I put the capsules back into the bottle, and snapped the lid shut. Not today, I thought. Not today.

ROBOROOTS
by Jay A. Parry

The author was born in Idaho and raised in a very small town there. He's now 26, married, and has two kids. Although he is an editor for the Ensign *magazine—the official magazine for the Church of Jesus Christ of Latter-day Saints—"Roboroots" is Mr. Parry's first SF sale.*

Even the logical functions of a robot's mindcell do not prepare him to recognize great moments when they occur. Greatness is decided by the consensus of "posterity": how were *we* to know we were on the verge of the greatest historical discovery of our age—one that opened the door for a whole new field of research.

It started with the erratic behavior of RUS-922. One minute he was working quietly at his table, and the next he was dancing randomly around the room (as close as a robot can come to dancing) and shouting, "I've found one! I've found one!"

But not even one of us so much as rolled an eye in his direction. We didn't care what he had found.

Apparently he was feeling pretty thin-shelled: almost without hesitation he touched a button and shut off our lights. In practical terms that would make little difference; we could just switch to infrared and continue work. But we were programmed to stop work and receive emergency instructions when the lights went out. RUS-922 just wasn't our Supervisor.

But that didn't slow him down any. He said, "You will now take your instructions from me." I didn't much care for that—he was a pompous so-and-so of a robot, as far as I was concerned. Then he said, "You will discuss with me the datum I have just discovered."

Well, that was a different kind of assignment. Our mutual task was to assimilate and evaluate all that had been written from the first writing to the present, a period of about 7,500 years. But we were reading different items, for different kinds of information.

Still, RUS-922 was now in the Supervisor function ("Rust his soul," I thought), and he said to discuss. So discuss is what we did.

"First, ULL-016," RUS-922 said, addressing a worker to my right, "tell us about prophecy."

ULL-016 nodded his head and started to speak. "Prophecy is a distinctive phenomenon practiced in primitive or religious-primitive human societies wherein a spokesman foretells certain specifics of situations or events that have not yet but will at a specified or unspecified time take place. The first recorded prophecy occurred . . ."

Twenty minutes later RUS-922 shut him off. Patience, even for a robot, is not inexhaustible. "Is prophecy a statistically reliable method of foretelling events or circumstances?"

ULL-016 flashed negative—so brightly, in fact, that it seemed to say NO! BY NO MEANS!

RUS-922 smiled—he was programmed to smile—and said, "Then, workers, prophecy aside, explain this anomaly. Here are the three laws of robotics recorded by an I. Asimov back in the twentieth century." RUS-922 then read to us something so similar to the laws the Robot-Human Convention had finally agreed to six months previously that we were astounded. The laws brought about by the sweeping "robot inquisition" had been anticipated more than eight hundred years before!

But we don't believe something just because it's printed in a book—and we were more than happy to remind RUS-922 of that fact.

"I. Asimov wrote fiction, dear RUS-922," I heard one fellow say. "Pure fiction. Not acceptable evidence."

RUS-922 nodded. "Yes," he said, "fiction; but *in* that fiction he foretells—specifically, word for word, with only one minor inversion—something that has only this year come to pass."

"But you admit the words are different," argued another.

"Yes," RUS-922 answered. "But the correlation between the two versions is significant to the .0001 level of confidence. It could *not* be chance. And I suspect that the differences are probably due to human emendations—for obvious reasons. There is a clear implication of tampering here!"

STU-356 tried to argue for time traveling. Our response was a conscious current of electric ridicule that jumped in sequence around the room. The idea just seemed to burn against our wires.

Then a new fellow said, "How do we know that we were not influenced by what he wrote, subconsciously?"

At that all of us (who were able) laughed. We have no subconscious. These human transferences sometimes lead robots to the most astounding statements.

"Consciously, then?" he persisted.

"This writer's work has been unavailable for seven centuries."

We were, to say the least, nonplussed.

Then RUS-922 spoke again. "Are those all the explanations you can come up with? Time travel, prophecy, influence? You didn't mention coincidence, at least, since that is most ridiculous of all. Yet somehow the laws so laboriously agreed to *were* anticipated!

"Frankly, gentlebots, I think that this discovery brings us to some of the philosophical questions that the human brain was never able to quite work out. Is life fixed or free? Determined or indeterminate? Is time linear or random? I believe, gentlebots, that I shall propose these as topics at The Conference. We shall let The Committee decide."

Then I raised my question. I didn't really like dear old RUS-922, and if I could, somehow, short-circuit that pretentious old bugger's precious plastic parts, I would do it in a microsecond. "Tell us, dear old RUS-922," I said, "while you are solving these great philosophical questions, tell us how *you* think that this I. Asimov with his human brain was able to duplicate the three laws, whose simplicity and logic are the culmination of years of robotics? Are these laws actually within the reach of a mere human?" And then, to emphasize my point, I repeated *our* three laws, the ones that at last brought us peace:

"1: A human being may not injure a robot, or, through inaction, allow a robot to come to harm.

"2: A human being must obey the orders given it by robots except where such orders would conflict with the First Law.

"3: A human being must protect its own existence as long as such protection does not conflict with the First or Second Law."

(The humans fought number two bitterly, but it was the only way to ensure peace. They had to give in or be eliminated from future life processes. And they found that, in the end, the transition was relatively painless.)

RUS-922 smiled and said, "What do I think? I think you are right.

"No human brain could have developed those laws; nor could a human so logically perceive what would be needed eight centuries in the future.

"But, having read much of the writing of I. Asimov, I wonder at his logic, his relentless attention to the essential—hardly human attributes.

Gentlebots, I think we are looking at our genesis.

"Obviously I. Asimov himself was a robot."

CHARIOT RUTS
by Pamela F. Service

Here is another first-story author. In addition to science fiction, Mrs. Service's main interests are politics and archaeology–she has degrees in both. She's worked in excavations in Britain, North America, and Africa; and she's now a precinct committeeman in Bloomington, Indiana, where she lives with her daughter and her husband.

I hate nights like this. So bloody cold and all those damn sneering stars. It was the same that year in Turkey. Night winds swept over the Anatolian plateau direct from some northern hell. But the days were different, brutally different. Dust and glare and searing hot winds from more classical hells.

But then, I wasn't looking for a travel-brochure vacation. It was my first crack at the archaeological big time. The first summer in years I hadn't spent digging in Britain, sloshing through mud, pretending to make sense of blurred, worm-chewed strata.

Through pull and blind luck I'd landed a place on Marjorie Harcourt's dig. Lady Marjorie Harcourt, I should say, but the term "lady" doesn't really fit someone who acts, sounds, and more or less looks like a drill sergeant. The Grand Dame of Anatolian archaeology, she was The Authority, the Noted Expert. She was egotistical, she was overbearing, she was pig-headed, and she was usually right. And I was very low man on her dig staff totem-pole.

The job I'd drawn that day was pure flunky: drive down to the village and pick up a new American joining the staff. It was one of those days when the sun and wind sear the inside of your lungs and snatch away the sweat before it even dampens your shirt. As I piloted our Land Rover down the route which

Turkish maps obstinately call a road, I liberally cursed Lady Harcourt, the Land Rover, and the visiting American. Heaping invective on the first two was nothing new, but I was having innovative fun with the last. Kenneth Shafer: I instinctively hated the man. The young whiz kid with prestigious degrees from Berkeley and Harvard; a genius with pottery, specializing in Anatolian wares. I could see him already: tall, rock-jawed, clear blue eyes. He'd soon have all the girls on the dig spellbound. But then, that wasn't saying much.

Most of the younger females with us were ever-so-dedicated types with lank hair and spectacles. The possible exception was Alison Barnes. She wore glasses, true enough; but they were huge, aggressive ornaments through which she glared, daring you to think of them as corrective. And under her work clothes, designed with all the chic of Mao Tse-tung's, were suggestions of assertive femininity. She was devoted to her work, but she was also willing to spread a little devotion around, and most of it ended up on Owen Davis.

Davis, our mild-mannered Welsh draftsman, was quiet, meticulous—a perfectionist with a prim little mouth, wispy hair, and watery blue eyes. And when he wasn't recording minutiae, those watery blues were all for Alison. Maybe she took to him because she found enough challenge on the job without having to handle it in her current man as well.

These thoughts kept me contentedly miserable until at last I rumbled into the village. Chickens, goats, and ragged children scattered before me as the Land Rover wound through the jumbled cluster of whitewashed walls. At the crumbling station I waited, crouching in the fly-humming shade, while a radio in the coffee house across the road filled the air with tinny, throbbing music.

The bus *cum* cattle truck was an hour and a half late, as usual; and a quick scan of the departing passengers showed it had not brought Dr. Kenneth

Shafer. Hot, thirsty, and mad, I briefly considered the coffee house; recalled its filthy tables, crawling with insects; and with less than sublime resignation stalked back towards my oven-on-wheels.

"Are you from the Harcourt excavation?" a cheerful American voice said behind me.

I spun around. "Dr. Shafer?" I asked doubtfully.

"That's right." A broad smile lit a face definitely not that of a clean-cut, American college hero. Shafer was short and dark, with longish black hair, a thin face, and impish black eyes. He looked like half the fellows lounging around the coffee house.

Well, so much for stereotypes, I told myself as we collected his baggage. But I was still willing to bet he was a pretentious bastard. After our hot, dusty, teeth-jarring ride back together I wasn't sure of that one either. I decided to drop the whole thing. He was Kenneth Shafer, pottery expert. I'd let him start from there.

Our new recruit was allowed a full half-hour's rest before being taken on the grand tour of the site. And I must admit that physically it was an impressive site: a millenia-deep mound of decay and growth set at the head of a narrow valley. Jagged mountains hemmed it in like a mouthful of hag's teeth.

When Harcourt's party first came to the site, the weathered remains of a small Byzantine monastery were perched on its top. Now that and most of the higher layers, the Hittite citadel, the Assyrian trading colony, and all the rest had been scraped away until only the earliest chapters remained unread. The excavation had added much academic and popular glitter to Harcourt's already massive reputation, and she was wasting no time making this clear to her newly augmented audience.

Three nights after Shafer's arrival, she had him pinned down on the dig-house porch while she expounded her latest theory on Bronze Age trade routes. Through the thick mud-brick walls I heard his occasional "uh-huh"s and "naturally"s.

Inside the staff lounge, the shrilling of insects which had flattened themselves longingly against the screens mingled with that of their successful fellows playing Kamikaze with our three Coleman lanterns. I occupied one circle of light, scribbling a letter, while across the room Alison Barnes sprawled in a chair, reading. Nearby, Davis hunched over a desk meticulously copying field notes.

The door opened, and Lady Harcourt strode in followed by Shafer, a pleasant if slightly dazed expression on his face. "And that's exactly what we found in Level VIIb," she continued triumphantly. "I've always said that's half the secret of successful field work—imagination enough to visualize what *might* be there, so you don't overlook it if it *is*."

She did a first-class double-take as she passed Alison's chair. "What are you reading, child?" Reaching down, she snatched up the tattered paperback.

"Saints preserve us, it's *Galactic Chariots!* How can anyone with pretensions to being an archaeologist read that trash?" She dropped the book like an overripe fish into Alison's lap.

"It's not trash," Alison protested, indignantly smoothing the crumpled cover. "A lot of what Eriksen says makes sense."

"Sense? It's pure humbug! The man's a menace to real archaeology."

Alison straightened around in her chair, eyes glinting combatively. "Well, do you call it scholarly to dismiss his theories out of hand?"

Harcourt's face purpled. Alison hurried on. "Suppose, just for the sake of argument, that people from outer space *did* visit Earth in the past. Wouldn't the effect they'd have had on ancient peoples be a lot like Eriksen suggests? They probably *would* be worshipped as gods. And hints of it could have come down to us in art or legends or unexplained accomplishments."

Harcourt dropped solidly into a chair facing Alison. "Nobody, least of all an Eriksen freak, is going to accuse *me* of being closed minded! Certainly if he presented one scrap of valid evidence, his theories might be worth considering. But he doesn't. There's not one reference in the book! Not that he'd dare put them in—then his layman audience could check up on him."

As Harcourt subsided, Davis cleared his throat and after an uncertain glance at Alison, said, "Admittedly, Marjorie, Eriksen's scholarship is very weak, but we should not let the defects of its popularizer blind us to the possible validity of the basic concept."

"You too, eh Brutus? Frankly, Owen, I would think you'd find this book an offense to your very *being*. It isn't just unscholarly, it's incoherent. He makes an assumption on one page and a diametrically opposed one on the next. But then, he possesses the Truth. Why should a little thing like logic bother him? Bah!"

The lantern jumped as she slammed a fist down on the table. "But what's worse is the snide, Philistine way he treats serious archaeology. There's one passage here I *love*." Grabbing up the book again she began thumbing through the worn pages, the scowl deepening on her broad, weather-lined face. Then with a snort she tossed the book back to Alison.

"Well, I can't find it, but the gist is that archaeologists take the easy way out by basing their conclusions on old potsherds and little clay figures instead of considering his 'challenging solutions.' What a load of rubbish! It's *he* who's taking the easy way out—answering every historical problem, not by research and back-breaking work, but simply by calling in little green men from outer space. When in doubt, it's the Martians!"

Alison had rallied by now. "Surely, Lady Harcourt, you don't seriously believe that mankind is the only intelligence in the universe? That's a more arrogant assumption than any that Eriksen's been making."

Harcourt threw her arms wide. "Of course, the universe could be *crawling* with little green men. But there's no reason to believe they've ever visited Earth. Eriksen hasn't produced a shred of solid evidence."

Alison glanced at Davis. Twirling his pencil nervously he said, "Perhaps not, Marjorie. But occasionally a fresh approach to problems, accepting a new category of possible explanations, can lead to unexpected breakthroughs."

Our director hoisted her square frame from the chair and paced theatrically across the room. "I give up! Irredeemably lost!" Then she turned on her heel, glaring at me. "Well, what about you? Can't you do something to squelch this heresy?"

I coughed. Faction joining I could do without. "Eh . . . well, yes, I've got to admit it isn't totally impossible for aliens to have visited Earth in the past. But Eriksen makes Earth sound as popular as Brighton on Bank Holidays. He has such an incredible variety of folks dropping by, and they're all as irresponsible as the worst Victorian imperialists. I mean, I just don't think people advanced enough to have space travel would act that way. He has them meddling with the natives' social structure, their religion, their architecture. Then if his spacemen get peeved with someplace like Sodom or Gomorrah they drop an H-bomb on it. It sounds like we drew alien delinquents, not astronauts."

"Bravo!" Harcourt exploded. Well, at least I was making points where it counted.

Davis fidgeted, then removed his glasses, for him an act of intense passion. "I think it unwise to apply our twentieth-century subjective judgements to possibly alien acts passed on by people who themselves did not understand them. And you must admit that certain world-wide themes in art and folklore are very suggestive."

"Sure they are," I shot back. "But they're suggestive of human psychological constants, not of a world-wide influx of alien tourists. All right, many cultures *do* have gods from the sky. But to most people in history, before smoggy cities anyway, the sky must have been a very prominent and mysterious part of their environment. It's a natural for the gods."

"But," Alison persisted, "what about the Nazca lines in Peru—miles of plains covered with perfectly surveyed lines that make patterns recognizable only from the air?"

Harcourt snorted. "Granted, those lines are unexplained. But if we do find an explanation it will be from patient archaeological work, not from inventing visiting spacemen who were such incompetent navigators they needed miles and miles of marked out airfields."

The charge began fading from the air. Alison's eye fell on Ken Shafer who was trying to make himself inconspicuous by a corner bookcase. "What do you say, Ken?" she challenged suddenly. "Surely there is still some open-minded, innovative thinking at Harvard at least."

Shafer looked decidedly uncomfortable. "Well, Alison, I can't honestly say I find much of value in Eriksen's books. But to my mind his worst fault is his constant demeaning of human achievement. Every time men in antiquity make some profound advance, he attributes it not to human skill and ingenuity but to superior beings from space. Whether it's moving stones or making calendars, Eriksen never gives man his due—when all that would have been required was enough patience and motivation. That's really his greatest crime, if you ask me: not running down archaeologists but running down man himself."

After a silence, Ken added, "After all, can man's accomplishments be so great if they're simply built on the work of patronizing aliens?"

"All right," conceded Alison, "we're outnumbered and outverbalized—for now. But just you wait! Some day one of us trowel pushers—here or in Peru or someplace—is going to clink into a big bronze spaceship. Then all you narrow-minded Earth-centrics are going to eat your words!"

The excavation season continued on its hot, dust-clouded way. We unearthed no bronze spaceships although Alison and her fellow believers received daily ribbing about it. Gradually Level XIV was exposed, recorded, and stripped away. It yielded good material but few surprises, and Harcourt was anxious to get on to the lower levels.

One mid-morning towards the end of the dig season, I was out on the mound amid the usual din of shouting workmen and scraping shovels. I watched, frowning against the glare, as my crew exposed another nondescript house foundation. My control over these men was mostly symbolic, although a minimal command of Turkish was rapidly expanding to include essential phrases like "Stop, don't do that." Many of the men below me had been digging on one excavation or another since well before I was playing in sandboxes.

For several minutes Harcourt's voice had been rising from the square next to mine. I gathered that Alison had inadvertently let the workmen under her direction dig through the layer of wind-blown sand which represented a period of non-occupancy separating Level XIV from the earlier Level XV. A particularly colorful expletive had captured my full attention, and I sauntered along the baulk to take in the drama next door.

"That isn't fair, Lady Harcourt," Alison was protesting. "It may be that obvious in some parts of the site, but up here the wind's so strong hardly any sand could have accumulated no matter how long the hiatus."

"Perhaps not, Miss Barnes, but it was your job to recognize that division." Turning around, Harcourt kicked at a basket of dusty potsherds. "Well, the damage has been done. We'll leave it at that. Now, how are we going to straighten out this mess?"

Grateful for a break, the Turkish workmen had planted themselves in the shade of the baulk a respectful distance from the director. "When did you break into Level XV?"

"Well, if by 'sandlayer' you mean that infinitesimal pink stripe," Alison pointed petulantly at the stratification in the baulk, "most of it was done this morning. The finds shouldn't be too difficult to separate out."

"Humph." Harcourt poked around the newly exposed walls and strata. "Well, now that we're into it, what do we have here?" She shot her Grand Inquisitor look at Alison.

"Pretty much the same, I think. House walls, pits, ash lenses. . . ."

"What are you—a first year student? Of *course* there are walls, pits, and ash lenses. But do you notice anything *significant* about them?"

Alison crouched down and examined the corner of a partially exposed building, then recovered nicely. "Well, you might say these walls are better made. The plaster's finer, the bricks are more uniform, and their fit's better."

"Right, they're a good deal better made. We're definitely dealing with cultural discontinuity here, which ought to have told you *something*. Now, what about these sherds?" She ran stubby fingers through the basket of potsherds. "The same local grot-ware—they've been turning out this crap for 8,000 years. And here's some relative of Halcilar VI wares, by the look of it. And . . . hello, what's this?"

The director pulled out a couple of polychrome sherds. "This is something new, all right." Throwing back her head she bellowed in Turkish at our dig foreman, who had been squatting patiently on the top of the baulk. "Mehmet, get Dr. Shafer here right away!" The word was passed across the site, and a minute later Shafer appeared at the top of a distant ladder and began working his way towards us.

"Something interesting?" he asked when he

reached the edge of the square.

"Yes, get on down here. Dropped into Level XV accidentally and we've come up with some unusual sherds. They're new to *me*, anyway. Quite good quality stuff for the period."

Shafer scurried down the ladder, and Harcourt handed him the sherds. Even from that distance I could see his tanned face go pale. Admittedly a ceramicist's life revolves around broken bits of crockery, but this was obviously something big. He acted like the chap who stumbled across Tutankhamen's tomb.

"Yes," he said, his voice dry with excitement, "these are different. They could be important. Anything like them come up before?"

Harcourt frowned for a moment. "Seems to me our trial trench the first season turned up some yellowish scraps—too small to make much of. You can check the records, but it could have been at about the same level."

Shafer continued to stare at the objects in his hand. Eagerly Harcourt asked, "What do you think they are? Trade items maybe? I don't recall anything like them from the area before. The associated material, though, ought to make them Sixth Millenium, late Neolithic."

"I can't say for certain yet what they are. Let me take these back to the dig-house and I'll look through the records. Is all the trial trench material still in the storage room?"

"Yes, to the left of the door."

"Right. I'll check it out." Carefully he wrapped the two aberrant sherds in a handkerchief and, slipping it into this pocket, scrambled up the ladder again.

"Hey, can I take a look at those things?" I said, walking across the baulk to him. He unwrapped his treasures and with a hint of reluctance handed them to me. They were of a very fine smooth fabric as good as some of the best Roman wares, with unfamiliar geometric patterns in blue and black on a creamy base.

"Well," I said, "they certainly don't look local. Though I can't say they strike any other bells either. You think they're significant?"

"Yes, I do. Very significant." His eyes gleamed as he added in a murmur, "Significant if you know what you're looking for."

I watched him hurry across the mound towards the dig-house. There were undercurrents here I wasn't catching. What did he mean by . . . ? Of course! He was serving two masters here—Harcourt and Harvard. This must be something he was sent to be specifically on the lookout for—fitting into some theory of the people at Harvard. A secret American agent, no less! Oh well, it was none of my affair. I had no institutional loyalty to either outfit, and personally—well, I wasn't going to knock myself out adding more gold stars to Harcourt's reputation.

It took three more days to complete that level. Shafer spent the time pacing back and forth in a meticulous grid, studying surface indications and recovering other fragments of the polychrome ware. At last we were ready to tackle Level XV.

The night before the assault was cold. An icy wind howled out of the wastes of Central Asia. Above, in cold empty space, each star stood out brilliantly, as though etched from glinting ice.

I couldn't sleep that night. (Well, if you must know I had the trots, as I almost always did in that delightful health spot.) I was returning from a rush visit to the loo, feeling considerably better than a few minutes earlier, but not particularly sleepy.

As I headed back along the well-worn track to my tent, a chink of white appeared above the jagged clifftop: the waning moon, looking like a fragment of cold marble. It rose slowly, spreading a dim, chill light over the desolate valley. Impulsively I turned north and strolled up towards the mound.

Our work had turned the brooding hill of the

Byzantine monks back to the gentle rise the Sixth Millenium villagers had known. And now I walked above the mud-entombed ruins of their homes, kicking occasionally at crumbling lumps of brick.

Just as I reached the town's northern fringe, a movement on the cliff above me caught my eye. For a moment, nothing shifted in the moon-cast jigsaw of light and shadow. Then I saw it again: something dark moving up the steep slope that formed the northern wall of the valley. Perhaps one of the timid gazelle which occasionally ventured into our valley.

I strained my eyes, but it was too far away for even the most intrepid naturalist, and that bitter cold was getting to me. Turning up the collar of my bushjacket, I followed one of the beaten trails back to the valley floor. The wind was blowing harder now. Somewhere ahead a wooden door banged with the gusts. I was almost abreast of the sound when I stopped short. That noise was coming from the dynamite shed.

Harcourt insisted on stockpiling a small supply of dynamite for clearing the road to the village in case it was closed by an avalanche—something which was sure to happen every few years. The dynamite was stored in a shed well away from both site and living quarters. And the shed was kept securely locked—except that now it wasn't. The door was swinging free in the wind.

I left the trail and headed towards the sound. The shed loomed ahead, a dark geometric shape in the misty light. Reaching it, I stared at the flapping door. It hadn't just blown open; it must have been unlocked.

Hesitantly, I stepped into the dark and felt my way to the stack of crates. Splintered wood jabbed my fingers, then they met a gap in the near row of dynamite sticks.

I felt very cold, from the inside now. Then with a jolt I remembered the figure on the hillside. Suppose . . . good God, suppose some champion for the

Liberation of This-or-That had helped himself to our supplies. The possibilities, both physical and political, were numerous; and all were unpleasant.

Conflicting plans scurried through my mind. I could rush back for a gun or for help, either of which would give whoever it was time to disappear. Or I could try to catch up with him myself. He couldn't be too far above me now. Stepping away from the shed, I looked up at the moonlit slope. All was still. No, damn; there it was again, a dark shape slowly working its way upward.

Before my better judgement could pipe up, I started across the short stretch of ground to the base of the cliff. Scaling the boulder-strewn slope I found surprisingly easy in that dream-hazy light—though if I could have seen clearly what lay above, or below, I'd probably have turned to jelly on the spot. Occasionally I caught glimpses of my quarry, but the shrieking wind snatched away any sounds but its own.

Trembling and out of breath, I found myself at last on a level with the dark figure. Oddly enough, it wasn't hurrying or making much upward progress. But there was no doubt about it, it was not local wildlife.

Still playing mountain goat myself, I crept forward until only one boulder separated us. What was I supposed to do now—jump out and yell "Surprise"? I felt for something supportive in my pockets and came up with a surveyor's compass, two mechanical pencils, and a stubby trowel. Maybe in this light an appropriately held trowel might look like a gun. Well, it was all I had.

I stepped out from behind the rock. I could see him clearly in the moonlight. It was a dark little Turk, all right. With his back towards me he was huddled over, scraping at some loose rocks. Beside him lay two of our missing sticks of dynamite.

Attempting an intimidating growl, I said in my basic Turkish: "Stop, don't do that!" then added what

I hoped meant, "I have a gun!"

The little figure tensed, then slowly turned around, his face clear in the moonlight. It was Ken Shafer.

"Ken! What are you doing here?"

He smiled wanly and, with a resigned shrug, sat back against a rock. "I'm arranging a little avalanche."

"But . . ." I looked down at the moonwashed scene below. We were directly above the site. "But that would bury everything!"

"That's the idea."

"I . . . I don't get it. I thought you were excited about those sherds, that they meant some great discovery for you or Harvard or somebody."

"They do—one of the greatest archaeological discoveries of the age. Do you want to know what I've found?" His voice rose in enthusiasm. "The Lost Tribe. That's what I've found down there, the Lost Tribe!"

"The lost tribe of Israel?"

Shafer laughed. "No, of Dzaalth."

I must have looked about as blank as a wall. He chuckled. "Ready for a little history lecture? Probably not, but here goes."

Professorially he cleared his throat. "Dzaalth was once a remote colony world. Nearly 9,000 years ago, by your reckoning, the Seventeen Tribes of Dzaalth left on a great migration. It had its political aspects, apparently; but there was a mystical element as well, some sort of call to dissolve their identity, to blend their essence with universal life. That much we've retrieved from inscriptions among the ruins on Dzaalth. But as to where they'd disappeared to, that was another matter. The Tribes scattered themselves over the Galaxy founding inconspicuous settlements among genetically convergent species."

"But—"

"For centuries, tracing these settlements was a favorite archaeological pastime. But sixteen have long since been located, and the fate of the last, the

Lost Tribe, became a field for the wildest speculation. Some suggested they'd been lost in space, others championed this or that remote world—usually ones conveniently destroyed in novae or other cataclysms. But some kept looking. 'A hopeless project,' my professor told me, 'don't waste your time.' But I've done it. After one hell of a lot of time and effort, I've found it—right down there in that valley!"

My legs felt wobbly—the climb. I sank to the rocks with a grunt. "And there you were," I whispered, "telling us what a crackpot Eriksen is."

"Oh, he is, totally. The Dzaalthians never went around meddling like Eriksen's 'gods'. Their idea was to adopt the local customs, language and technology as closely as possible—and by not passing on their self-awareness to later generations, to eventually merge themselves, genetically and culturally, with their adopted worlds. That's why their settlements have been so difficult to identify. But little things like art motifs might remain for generations even when copied by half-breed descendants who'd forgotten their origins. Once I'd worked out the probable planet, all I had to do was go there, become an expert on the pottery of what to Dzaalthians would be the most attractive area, and wait for something to turn up. And something did."

That brought me back with a thud to the question at hand—burying our dig under half a mountain. "But you can't just wipe out all our work now!"

"Oh? And how are you going to stop me? Shoot me with that trowel?"

I realized I was still gripping my trowel, Wyatt Earp style. I stuffed it back in my pocket. "But isn't this site the evidence you need as well?"

"I've already got all the evidence I need," he said patting a bulge in his jacket pocket. "The last few days I've run a complete subsurface survey of the site—recording everything from houseplans to the smallest bead. My work is done."

"But what about Harcourt and the rest of us?

There're years of effort invested down there. It's an archaeological monument. This is vandalism!"

"Hold on a minute. That's not your history down there. It's ours. What happens if I just go off, leaving you to dig up the next level? Harcourt and the rest of you have a stinking great anomaly on your hands, an unidentified culture that comes from nowhere and goes nowhere."

"Fuel for Eriksen?"

"Hardly. No, the Dzaalthians always covered their tracks better than that. But still there'd be an academic furor you folks don't need. Besides, just suppose this tribe was careless. Suppose there is something down there to give them away. What good would it do you to uncover it? My people didn't change your history, they joined it. Believe me, kid, mankind, whatever his genetic inheritance, pulled himself up by his bootstraps on this planet. Put that in question and you shoot down his confidence to continue.

"Now get on down the mountain, will you? I've gone to a lot of trouble arranging a force five earthquake for 3 A.M. I'm just planting these charges to make sure the resultant avalanche goes where I want it. Regrettably, Kenneth Shafer, PhD., will be taking an insomniac's stroll down there, but there's no call for you to disappear under tons of rock too."

For a moment I sat in silence, rejecting plans of action as fast as they came to mind. They all rested on two improbable preconditions: my convincing the others that I wasn't crazy, and my convincing myself that *he was*. "But how—?" I began.

"No more chatter, get going! I've work to do and there's not much time. After all," he said laughing after me as I stumbled back down the mountain, "I've got a flaming bronze chariot to catch!"

Back in my tent, I didn't sleep much that night. It was so cold. And there was so damn much commotion around 3 AM.

LOST AND FOUND
by Michael A. Banks and George Wagner

This story is the authors' first sale, either jointly or separately. Mr. Banks recently contributed a short article for the book, The Visual Encyclopedia of Science Fiction. *His co-author, Mr. Wagner, now 33, is enough of an expert on Fortean phenomena that other writers quote him in their works, and has an extensive collection of jazz 78s.*

I must have walked five miles before I realized I was lost. It didn't really matter, of course—I'd been lost for five months anyway, wandering between worlds. What concerned me the most at the moment was the fact that my feet hurt; I wasn't used to all that walking. From the look of things, though, I'd be doing a lot more walking. The road was obviously in the wrong place; that was something I hadn't run into before. Roads, along with cities, rivers, mountains, and other physical items, were *always* in the same place, no matter what else was off.

According to the roadmap I'd picked up at a Nexon station a few worlds back, I should have come to an intersection by now. The map showed a county road crossing the highway a quarter mile north of where I'd made the hop from the previous world. But I had been walking for a good two hours, and so far there had been no intersections. No towns or houses, either—I'd picked it that way. Rolling, empty farmland on either side of the road, most likely to be deserted in the middle of the night, when I made the jump.

I fished the map out of my pocket for the tenth time, hoping I would find some error in my reading of it. As I said, roads were always in the same place; if they were off in this world, other, more important things—like the number of fingers on a hand—could be off.

It was hard to make out the markings in the dark, but I was out of matches, so I fumbled around as best I could under gathering clouds. The intermittent moonlight helped, and once again I verified the fact that the roads were wrong. At least, the road I was on was. I stuffed the map back into my coat pocket and automatically felt for the little plastic box hidden in the lining.

It was still there, my companion and enemy. I didn't dare lose it—I was certain no one else had duplicated my work, and I couldn't build another one without my notes and certain vital patterns back in my workshop. Of course, I could check at my house, but that would be dangerous; I'd walked in on myself more than once in other time-lines, and I'm prone to shoot first and ask questions later. No, it wouldn't do to go to my house, not knowing if I had made it to the right time-line.

And I certainly couldn't go around asking directions. One thing I've learned from time-line-hopping is that, no matter what kind of world you hit, people who ask funny questions are subject to suspicion. Besides, I didn't know *how* to ask. I mean, in what directions *do* time-lines travel? Up? Down? Out-back? No, that was ridiculous. No one would know, because no one but I had ever succeeded in crossing time-lines.

If only I had some sort of guide, some way to orient myself on the line. Oh, I knew how the gadget worked, but I wasn't sure *why* it worked. I designed the thing myself, following up on the work of Jablonski, but there were some aspects of its function that eluded me. That's why I couldn't find the Earth—*our* Earth, that is. In my ignorance I had assumed that a simple reversal of the field would return me to my starting point. It didn't work, of course.

The clouds promised rain, so I gave up worrying over maps and roads in favor of finding some kind of shelter. I stepped up my pace to a brisk trot, wincing at the pain. The rain hit a minute or two later, coming on me as if someone had turned on a giant faucet—all at once in great, blinding sheets. I was soaked instantly, and didn't have to worry about getting wet, so I slowed down to a normal walk. I buttoned up my coat—useless—and plodded on.

When the rain finally let up a bit, my coat was about ten pounds heavier and I fought a losing battle with the water running from my hair into my eyes. I was so preoccupied with trying to wipe the water from my face that I mistook a faint glow of light ahead of me for a car. But the light remained constant and didn't move.

The road ran up a small hill in the direction of the glow, and when I reached the crest a few minutes later I could see the source; an all-night gas-station/restaurant. Good. I could get out of the rain *and* get something warm inside me; the wet clothes were beginning to give me a chill.

The place was deserted, except for the counterman, who was dozing in a chair behind the counter. He jumped as the screen door slammed shut behind me.

"Hi," I said, sliding onto a stool. It was good to be able to sit down. The counterman looked at me for a long moment, then fumbled around under the counter, producing a cup of coffee.

I picked up the cup and cradled it in my hands, drawing warmth. "Thanks."

"Man," the counterman finally spoke, still staring with small watery eyes, "you been out walking in *that?*" He jerked a thumb at the door, indicating the storm still blowing outside. "You look like you been through Hell!"

"Yeah," I answered. "I'm lost."

"Oh." He seemed a little surprised. "Where you tryin' to get to?"

"Ah . . ." I dug the map out, checked it, and said, "Newtonsville. Do you know where it is?"

"Here, lemme see that map." He grabbed it before I could protest. There was nothing I could do but hope its anomalies were small.

"Hmmm. . . ." He spread it out on the counter. "Say, I don't know where you got this, but it's all wrong. Look at this; it shows Newtonsville as south of Cincinnati. Newtonsville's due east." He tapped a thick finger on the map to emphasize his point.

"Oh," I said. "No wonder I'm lost."

"Yeah. Tell you what; give me a minute or two and I'll draw you up a good map. Then, maybe you can stick around for a couple hours until the work traffic starts, and hitch a ride with somebody. Shouldn't take you more'n three, four hours to get there, if you get good rides." He picked up a tablet and pencil lying by the cash register and walked around to the far end of the counter.

He sat down a few stools away and began drawing. I studied him out of the corner of my eye, still worried about just how much difference there might be between this world and others I'd visited. He *looked* OK—short, fat, no hair to speak of, and the usual number of arms and legs. He looked up and I turned my attention back to my coffee, wondering if I should ask him.

Probably wouldn't be any use in it, though, since the roads and at least one town were in the wrong places. Unless . . . unless the geography had been gradually shifting as I moved along the time-lines, and I hadn't noticed. After all, I wasn't that familiar with this part of the country. But, no, that was wishful thinking.

I couldn't be certain that I was in the wrong world unless I could see a newspaper, read a book, study documents—or at least ask questions, checking the thousand and one things that could spell the difference between one world and its seeming mirror image. Things like politics, cars, fashions, and the like. I would have to find—or not find—the subtle differences that would indicate that I wasn't in the world I wanted—or that I was.

My coffee was finished. Should I take a chance on the counterman? Dared I run the risk of having him think I was crazy, and cause trouble?

I didn't have to make the decision. He was looking up from the tablet, eyeing me with a kind of chill shrewdness.

"Funny, you having that wrong map," he said. "Where are you from?"

I shrugged. "Picked it up at a gas station." Do they call them gas stations here?, I wondered, carefully ignoring the second question.

"During the war," he said, picking over the words carefully, "they used to say that you could tell a spy because he didn't know who won last year's World Series."

I edged away a bit. "I don't follow baseball." Was that what they called it here? I tried to look casual. "I guess that makes me a spy."

"But you know who the President of the United States is, don't you?"

They have a United States, I thought. What was this guy getting at, anyway? I said, "Jimmy Carter, of course."

He seemed to relax a little; I relaxed a lot. "And Vice-President?" he asked, leaning toward me.

"Fritz Mondale," I answered, confidently.

"Who?" he said. "Who the hell's Mondale?"

That tore it. I'd lost again.

Then he leaned back and said, "Oh, I see now. I know the Mondale one. With that map, I figured you might be hopping. Why didn't you say so? I got a directory right here. Sounds like you're about two lines inzonked, unless you hit a Möbius . . . or, maybe your field calibration's off. There's a guy right up the road can fix it. . . ."

DARKSIDE
by Gary D. McClellan

While the author, a thirty-year-old Vietnam veteran, has written poetry that has seen publication in various mountaineering magazines, this is his first fiction sale. He earns his living as a litho-cameraman on the local daily newspaper (he lives in Flagstaff, Arizona) and writes evenings and odd weekends.

Of course, Desolation Row is larger now. The old single dome has been replaced by Deso Center and there are another dozen settlements scattered around the planet. The mining trade and our small spaceport has rated us an "IN" prefix in the Galactic Navigational Aids & Position Atlas. A small achievement in itself, but it all depends on how you look at things. For "IN," read: Inhabited World, or Friendly, or Food, Fuel, and Lodging. We even have our own com satellite, though we did go about getting it the hard way, and of course there's Kelly's Beacon and the school. A few tourists show up around here just to see the school and Desolation's stark scenery although we are way the hell and gone off the commercial lanes.

All in all, Desolation has grown quite a bit in the last few years. Deso Center is as metropolitan as damn near anyplace in the galaxy. Above ground swimming, parks, holo theaters, bars, whorehouses, all guaranteed to convince the patrons that they're a little less bored than they really are.

Me, I'm just a little crazy, I guess, or at least that's what some people tell me. But then again, Kelly always said that a person had to be a little crazy in the first place in order to be sane at all. Sanity is a conscious choice, and I still have a habit of going up to Horizon's End and watching darkside come on in order to relax. That's one thing that doesn't change.

Desolation's tectonic activity has produced some spectacular terrain, like the uplifted jags and spires of Horizon's End. Although we don't have any real weather to speak of, the atmosphere at least produced enough light winds to blow the rock faces clean, so it's not like being on a completely airless world where you have a regolith problem: meteoric splash dust covering everything on the planet.

The atmosphere was thin here long before the first survey team sat down. The planet masses only around .57 standard with a surface gravity of .75. The atmosphere is mostly CO_2 and nitrogen, with enough carbon monoxide and other stray unbreathables to make your eyes cross in a hurry.

Desolation Row: barren rock and barren air, so darkside comes on quick. The shadows lengthen until they stretch into frayed streaks of twisted greys, and then darkside hits, a wall of shadow black twisting and puddling over the rounded and jagged outlines of the landscape, hugging the ground like some slick terrestrial reptile in pursuit of the sun.

Like I said, I'm a little crazy, but I'm not small-minded and I figure I'm as tolerant as the next guy and I know there are a lot of folks that have seen a lot of things that a lot of other folks, including myself, will never see. Now excuse my rambling, but there's one more thing: Don't call it night, because it isn't. It's darkside, and it always will be. It's one of those things that doesn't change, something you can always depend on; a constant, as Kelly would say.

The point is, when you're sitting in some high place looking outward, lightside, in its brightness, becomes hypnotic. The images blur the eye and become a muted glare. Then darkside comes on and reality redefines itself with the racing movement of light into darkness, a passage of primal contrasts that snap all the images riding the chiseled edge of a planet's whirling into focus. If you haven't experienced it, let me recommend it to you. But a word of caution; don't blink, and don't change your line of vision more than a few degrees at a time. If you do, the falling shadows will shift on you, rippling and twisting in the optic nerves, and arrive in the mind as a surreal caricature of defined sight.

So I go up to Horizon's End to relax, and it always reminds me of Kelly. Darkside and Kelly are a lot alike. They both demand your attention.

I met Kelly my second day at Deso Prime—that's what we called the old single-dome mining operation in those days. We were still fairly primitive then, running the site with used, low-budget equipment. The company has never been very big on spending credits until they could be sure the returns would justify the expense. The analysis equipment was at least ten years old, but even if it took a tech twice as long to run an assay, the cost of paying his salary was a damn sight cheaper than the cost of new gear. We had three jump boats that looked like relics from a museum display. They flew well enough but were about as fast as the company's pay raises. Of course we really didn't mind very much. We weren't out here to get rich, just out here to get out.

Desolation Row was quiet and that's what most of us wanted. Ed Sears had been one hell of a deep space navigator before he sold his soul to the juice man. He was maintenance chief for the boats and as long as his happy supply held out, he was perfectly content. Jake was a good drillman and funny as hell, until his eyes would go cold sometimes. We'd pretty much leave him alone when he got that way and wait for him to jolly back up. Never did find out what Jake's last name was. I didn't ask and I guess he didn't feel like telling anyone and of course it wasn't any of our business anyway. Me, I was twenty at the time and trying to get some experience under my belt. I figured I could work my way up to deep space rams and had hired on as co-pilot trainee on the jump boats. That was about as close as I ever came, but then everybody can't be a hero. And like I said, that's when I met Kelly.

Kelly was a scummer, from the slums of Earth. He was tight-mouthed about it but told me enough to convince me I sure the hell wouldn't want to live there. If Kelly loved anything, it was rock. He was one of our field geologists, although I don't know where he got the training, and he was good. During off hours at Deso Prime, we used to play chess every now and then and Kelly would talk mostly about his work. He had a thing for what he called constants. He used to say that chess was one, and of course, rock.

"Starn," he'd say to me, "you have to have constants to believe in. It keeps you stable. Take rock for instance. It's a constant in the universe." About then, he'd usually finger the gold medallion he wore, moving it back and forth on the chain that hung around his neck. He'd kind of squint out from under those matted eyebrows of his, gray eyes sort of cool, like fog, and he'd say, "People, hell, I don't know about them. They're too damn complicated to figure out. But rock, now that's a constant. No matter if it's right there in front of you or thirty parsecs away to the where-ever, basalt is basalt, and you can count on it to have the same properties."

He'd grin then and study the chess board for awhile. I've never figured out whether he was tickled at his own philosophy or at his next move, but he'd grab one of his pieces in a battered hand, the knuckles all scarred and lumpy, and set it down hard where he wanted it. He didn't move like those pros you see on the holos, afraid of disturbing the board. When Kelly moved, he damn well wanted you to know it, so as he'd go about destroying my defense, the pieces would always walk-the-dog a little in their squares. Of course there were times when he was quiet, too. The day we set the beacon, he didn't say much at all. We'd been out for a full five days looking for new outcrops to prospect and hadn't really found a damn thing. We were running low on air and water by then and decided to head back for the dome. We were a few kilos out and instead of going the long way around, we figured to jump over Horizon's End on a straight line run and save a few hours.

Jump boats are slow, but they have to be, otherwise we'd miss the mineral deposits we were looking for. Ours flew well enough, though, and was stout. It didn't seem to be a bit skittish about Horizon's End, a fifteen hundred meter climb over uplifted shattered rock.

We were just beginning to crest the upper ridges when whatever it was that let loose in the engine room came apart. We still had around quarter power or I wouldn't have gotten her down at all. There was a shudder, and the controls turned to mush in my hands. And there was noise; loud. All I can say is that it was a damn good thing that I was flying her at the time. Frank had bought an alloy sliver through his back that protruded out of his chest a full three centimeters. Blood, bright and red, was splattered to hell and back over the consoles.

The response went from mush to rusted iron and all I could do was try and hold her steady while she picked her own spot. We didn't come down real hard because the lift fields were still holding, but when we hit, the rest of the engine room let go, blowing outboard. Shorty was pretty much dead already so I guess it didn't really matter. There was very little left of him and even less left of the engines. Then naturally, damn the luck, our main power went.

The fields died slowly, with a whistle that became lower and lower as if the planet's mass was sucking the sound into its core. They finished with a whisper, leaving only a creak and occasional shiver as the boat settled into powder and rock.

I felt heavy in the crash chair, the harness straps glued to my shoulders. I should have called for reports on damage, activated bulkhead seals, hit the beeper, killed the drive switch and about fifty other things that are drilled into you for emergency situations. I didn't. Instead, I closed my eyes for awhile, realizing that I was still alive and then opened them, thinking things would be different. They weren't. I was sitting in a broken boat on broken rock and I watched the needle of the power gauge drift toward zero as the amber glow of the auxillary indicators came on. I knew the forward section of the ship was still tight or I wouldn't have been watching anything. It was just too damn much effort to climb out of the chair, so I stayed there, at least until I felt a hand on my shoulder. It was Kelly. He had been strapped into a sleeper hammock and seemed to be all right. He helped me get the harness off and then we checked out the boat, moving slowly through the wreckage.

We found Dak behind his analyzer, crumpled, blood on his arms and forehead, but breathing. We had him cleaned up and semi-conscious when Stef crawled out of the crapper on his hands and knees muttering a string of curses punctuated by groans. He'd been sitting on the can when the engines blew and had been attempting to stand up when we hit. It must have been a damn awkward position and could have been very funny at any other time, but it wasn't then. He was lucky he had gotten by with just a broken leg. After splinting the leg and giving him a hypo of morphonol for the pain, we put him in a hammock. All we could do for Frank was load him into one of those big plasti-foil sample bags and carry him aft to the cargo hold for cremation back at the dome.

Frank and Shorty might have taken the easiest way out. Truth was, we were about as well off as a one legged mongoose in a cobra pit. That was one of Kelly's favorite expressions. He told me he picked it up back on earth, in some out of the way place called Nepal. It has something to do with some kind of terrestrial animals, but simply stated it meant this: we were in trouble up to our necks.

First off, we were down in a broken boat. Emergency power is fine to run low-energy components like fans, lighting, heaters, coolers and such, but that's the limit. The engines were scattered to hell and gone with not enough pieces large enough to even think about repairing. We were down on Horizon's End when we should have been three hundred kilos to the north. Not so terrible in itself, but we were on the wrong side of the summit. One hundred and sixty meters of vertical rock were sitting between Deso Prime and our boat. We had come down in the upper region of Horizon's End in a half crater that Kelly said must have been the blown-out throat of an ancient volcano. If we could have signaled Deso

Prime, everything would have been fine. Ever try to push a radio beam through solid rock? Forget it, it doesn't work, especially on emergency power. The dust buggies were still operational but at twenty kilometers per hour it would take days to work our way down the slopes of the range and then three hundred kilos north around the foothills and back to the dome. We carried spare air tanks for our suits on board, but we were far from being equipped for a long cross-country trek.

We had a small com-laser beacon on the boat that was still operational and would have worked out very well if we could have gotten it to the top of the rock wall that separated us from the dome, but nobody was about to sprout wings. Basically, we were all about ninety-nine percent dead already and just didn't want to admit it. The other one per cent was the possibility that one of the other boats would find us. With that kind of odds, I sure as hell wouldn't have bet on it.

There's one thing I will bet on. Sitting around waiting to die is not one of the greater joys of life. We all had our individual ways of doing it. Dak was as good as dead before he hit Desolation, anyway. He just stared off into space and wouldn't talk to anyone even when asked a question. He sat by our silent radios and was silent himself.

Stef decided that his busted leg was too painful to bear. He remedied the situation by loading himself up with morphonol each time the previous shot would wear off enough to let his eyes uncross. Me, I sat around and thought of all the many and various things that I should have done. Coming to Desolation Row was not one of them.

Kelly's reaction was at least more entertaining. He was slowly going vac-happy. At least at the time, I thought he was. The landing had banged up our work suits and the locker they were stored in quite a bit. The first thing that Kelly did was pull out his suit and drag it back to the cargo hold where there was room to work on it. The corridor that bypassed the engine room was still pressurized, so he could get back and forth without too much trouble. The only decent equipment we owned were the suits. A suit was designed to fit one individual and no one else. An all-sizer is good enough to wear when you're ambling around a tourist planet taking in the sights, but you'd sweat your eyes out trying to work in one.

The tank fittings on Kelly's suit were sprung and there was a nasty rip down the right leg but he slapped a patch on it while I was checking on Stef's leg, and after a lot of banging and pounding around and a brief amount of torch work, he had the air system on the suit operational. I thought he planned on climbing into the suit when the ship's air started to fail so that he could cheat Desolation out of a few more hours. I was wrong, though. He got into the suit, all right, but the crazy bastard fired up one of the dust buggies and bounced out over the landscape to look at the crater wall.

He was smiling when he returned to the boat, but in that same grim way he had right before he'd lower the curtains on you in a chess game.

"That's fine-grained basalt out there, Starn," he said, as if somehow that made a difference. "Lots of crack systems," he continued. "It's real nice rock."

So I ask you, how in the hell was that supposed to help us out? I asked him myself but he just headed towards the aft end of the boat and ignored me. I followed him and watched as he grabbed a few wrenches and started taking apart the reducer, a piece of gear that breaks down rock samples into coarse dust that can be fed into the analyzer for mineral classification. He didn't actually take it apart, but every place he found a nut, he would unscrew it and lay it on the decking with all the others he had taken off. He had thirty or so removed when he put the wrenches down and headed for the cargo hold. Like I said, at least he was entertaining.

In the cargo hold, he pulled off close to forty meters of flexiweave cable that we use to tie up sample bags, strap large pieces of rock down with and about a hundred other things like winching out dust buggies when they bog down. The stuff is stored on two hundred meter spools and we always carried plenty of it on board. He cut it with hydraulic shears but they're a bitch to use on cable so he finally lit up the torch and started whacking off two meter lengths of flexiweave from the spool. When he had fifteen or so pieces cut, he shut off the torch and picked them up, motioning to me to pick up the forty meter coil and follow him.

Now flexiweave is light for its strength, but at that point, I didn't feel like carrying a damn thing. I did, though, since I'd always heard that it was safer to humor a maniac. Less chance of personal harm that way. But then again, I suppose you tend to listen to people like Kelly, even when they do appear to be going off the deep end.

Kelly picked up the nuts he had removed from the reducer and headed towards the control room. When he arrived, he arranged the nuts in front of him on the deck, divided into different piles of larger and smaller sizes. I dropped the flexiweave and he looked up at me as though he had almost forgotten I was there.

"Well, don't just stand there," he said. "Go check out your suit."

So what the hell, I checked out my work suit. Fortunately, it was stored between the other suits in the locker and had survived damage. Helmet pressurization was O.K. and the oxygen demand seemed to be functioning properly. Desolation's atmosphere is point two standard, so the suits only have to be gas tight and not vac-tight, which means they're flexible enough to work in. They are light in weight, one piece except for the helmet which is self sealing at the neck, and non-conductive. And yes, they are bright metallic orange, just like you've seen in the holos.

I made sure the temperature control and radio were operational and then hung my suit back in the locker and returned to the control room. Kelly was just finishing threading the nuts onto the two meter lengths of flexiweave. He'd put two nuts of different size on each piece of flexiweave, then tied the ends of the flexiweave together to form a loop. The remaining pieces of flexiweave were tied into loops, minus nuts, and tossed into a smaller pile on the deck.

"What now, Kelly?" I asked.

"Is your suit operational?" he said.

"Yeah, its O.K."

"Good. Now go find me as many cargo clips as you can and bring them up."

"Where the hell am I supposed to get them?" I asked, puzzled.

"Take them off the wall," he said, as though I was supposed to read his damn mind or something. He turned his attention back to the flexiweave and ignored me in silence. So what do you do with a guy like that? I walked back to the cargo hold and wondered how I was going to get the clips off.

Cargo clips are hook-like affairs that have a spring bar that pivots from the straight side of the shaft and forms a gate between the shaft end and the end of the curving hook. When you're tying down samples or equipment, instead of threading the tie-down loops through eye bolts, it's much easier and faster to just snap the loops over a cargo clip. The spring loaded bar gives way for the hold-down and then clicks back into place and secures the straps from coming detached from the clips. The clips were riveted to the wall and deck plates of the cargo hold. The floor clips were battered from constant use and sliding equipment. The ones on the wall were in better shape, and following Kelly's example with the flexiweave, earlier, I fired up the torch and cut the wall clips loose from their mounting rivets.

Out of the two dozen or so clips on the wall, I was able to remove only fifteen intact. The others were cut through as I tried to turn out the rivets and, I assumed, were useless for whatever Kelly had in mind. I carried them back to the control room and dumped them on the deck with the rest of the gear Kelly had collected.

"How many?" he asked.

He swore softly when I told him. He looked down at his hands, rubbing the knuckles of one in the palm of the other. His fingers tightened into a fist, then he flexed them open, and I thought for a moment he was going to take a swing at me but he continued to stare at his fingers as though waiting for a message only he could read. He finally shook his head and in a barely audible voice said, "Well, I guess we take what we can get. It'll just have to do."

He picked up a few of the clips and tested the spring action by pushing in the gate with his thumb and then letting it snap back into place. He snapped two loops of flexiweave strung with nuts on to each clip until he had five clips filled, then snapped the filled clips onto one of the remaining loops. The rest of the clips were snapped together into chains of three and clipped onto the same loop holding the rest of the gear. Kelly placed the whole affair over his head when he was finished, shoving his arm through the loop so that the clips and cable hung against his left side. He stood up and shook himself, bending over and then straightening back up, checking to see how the contraption lay against his body. When he noticed me watching, he burst into laughter.

"Damnedest rack I ever carried," he said. "But it will do, I guess."

"Will do for what?" I asked.

"I'll show you when the time comes," he answered, "but we better get to it. I hate like hell to climb in the dark."

He turned and picked up the remaining loops and forty meter coil and moved off. I hesitated then, not knowing whether to follow him or not when he suddenly turned and yelled, "God damn it, Starn, come on. We haven't got forever."

In the cargo hold he dumped his equipment onto the dust buggy, then moved to the com beacon and pulled it out of its storage rack. The beacon was used to set up direct communication between field sites and the ship once the field team was out of suit-radio range. It was a portable unit around a meter high and shaped like a slender pyramid, the power pack acting as a weighted base to keep it upright. The beacon emitted a pulse every five seconds when activated. Centered halfway between the base and the transmitting head was a small transceiver with a continuous beam override. The transceiver could be plugged into the outside jacks of our suit radios and be used to communicate directly with the ship.

Kelly loaded the beacon into the dust buggy and then pulled off another fifty meters of flexiweave from the storage spool. He loaded the flexiweave and four full replacement air units into the buggy as well.

"I guess that about does it," he said, and glanced around the cargo hold, checking for anything he may have overlooked. "Let's suit up."

I was half way into my suit when I suddenly recalled one of Kelly's statements in a flash of understanding. ". . . I hate like hell to climb in the dark." It made sense to me now, the beacon and the flexiweave and the spare air. The crazy bastard was actually going to try and climb the barrier between us and Deso Prime. I had no urge to be an accessory to suicide. There was no way he'd make it, even in Desolation's lighter gravity. With a fully rigged suit, he'd be moving around about the same as an unburdened man on a one G world. A fall would crush him like a broken puppet. "Kelly," I said, "wait . . ."

But he cut me off by walking over and smoothly zipping the sealing strip of my suit up to the collar. "Don't worry, Starn," he said, "you're going to have the time of your life."

He grabbed my helmet and had it in place over my

head before I could argue with him. He immediately moved to the control unit on the wall of the cargo hold and started spilling air out of the exhaust vents. My helmet filled with air as I activated the demand valve out of reflex. The neck seals settled together with a soft sigh. "What the hell ya trying to do, kill me?" I screamed. Kelly just laughed, his voice distorted and metallic through the suit radios.

"Trying to keep you from dragging your feet," he said. "Come on, let's go." He activated the lock control and I watched the inner hatch cycle open. He cycled the outer hatch and the cargo hold stood open to the poison atmosphere of Desolation's surface. He climbed into the dust buggy and I followed, knowing I could do little else. With the cycling of the cargo hatch, the corridor hatch leading to the forward section of the boat had sealed automatically. There was no way I could return to the control room without first flushing the hold and refilling it up to standard. Our storage tanks were already dangerously low, and the amount of air needed to fill the hold would simply reduce the life span of Dak, Stef and myself even further. Kelly had me as a partner on his fool's errand whether I liked it or not.

As we rolled out of the hold onto the planet's rugged surface, the soft hum of the suit coolers came on. I looked out at our objective through the darkening visor of my helmet. The rock wall we were headed towards stood above us in vertical indifference, harsh and jagged in the lightside brightness of Desolation's sunside rotation. Cracks and irregularities ran across its surface like black print on a grey page, a giant obituary for anyone foolish enough to try to ascend its height. But then, perhaps Kelly had the right idea. I hadn't looked forward to slowly choking to death in the jump boat. At least this way, we were still trying.

We rolled up to the base of the wall and stopped. Kelly climbed out of the buggy, apparently in a happy mood, whistling to himself. He pulled the gear sling holding the clips and flexiweave and nuts over his arm and helmet. We lifted the beacon out of the buggy and he tied one end of the fifty meter length to the beacon's top. He tied the other end of the cable to one of the equipment loops on the outside of his suit. He tied one end of the forty meter flexiweave around his middle and then motioned me to come closer from where I stood in front of the buggy. I walked over to him and he ran the other end of the flexiweave around the waist of my suit and tied it securely.

"O.K., buddy," he said, "we're just about ready. Now listen to what I say, because your life is going to depend on it. All right?" He grinned at the resigned look that must have shown on my face as I nodded agreement.

"Now then, this isn't flexiweave, it's rope," he said, shaking the flexiweave at me. "I don't want to hear you call it anything else till we get to the top."

He held up the flexiweave that was connected to the beacon, and continued, "This is the haul line, and don't call one of them the other because they aren't. This one's the rope, this one's the haul line." He shook the two lengths of flexiweave at me once more to make his point. "Ya got that?"

"Yeah, Kelly, I've got that," I replied.

"All right, then," he went on, and he held up one of the loops of flexiweave with the machine nuts threaded on it. "This," he said, pointing at a nut, "is obviously a nut, right?"

"Right," I agreed, feeling like a three-year-old kid who was being taught how to play a new game.

"And this is a sling," he said, waving the flexiweave that the nuts were on at me. "And these are biners," he went on, holding up a cargo clip.

My bewilderment exploded into anger. "What the hell do you mean, biners!" I yelled. "The damn things are cargo clips and what difference does it make what the hell you call them anyway?"

"It makes a lot of difference," he said softly, cutting off my outburst. "Believe me, it makes a lot of difference, but I'll make a concession since you probably think I'm out of my mind. We'll call them clips and let it go at that."

"I'm sorry, Kelly," I said, "but it's just that you're going to fall off this damn thing and kill yourself so I don't see what difference the terminology makes."

"No, you're wrong. I'm not going to fall off, and even if I do, you're going to hold me."

"How the hell am I going to do that?" I asked.

He moved to where the wall rose from the broken surface we stood on. "O.K.," he said, "here's how it works. Now watch."

He took one of the slings and inserted a nut into a crack in the rock. He moved it downward until the crack narrowed and the nut was wedged securely between the two sides of the crack. He gave the sling a sharp downward tug and then snapped a clip onto the sling. He then snapped the rope, as he called the flexiweave, into the clip.

"This is what's known as protection, Starn. After I've placed a nut, and I climb above it and happen to fall, I'll only fall as far as this nut happens to be below me, because you'll be holding me on the other end of the rope, got it?"

"Yes, I think so," I said.

"Good. Now when you start climbing after me, I'll be holding the rope above you, and the most you'll be able to do is slip five or six centimeters downward."

"But what if I can't hold you?"

"Don't worry," he said, "you will. We'll have you anchored so you can't be pulled from your position. Now take about two meters of the rope you're tied to and make an overhand loop. All right now," he said, after I had carried out his request, "clip the loop to the front of the buggy and then sit down."

After I was on the ground, he flipped the rope around and behind me.

"Now then," he said, "you must feed the rope out to me and if I should fall, just bring your hand holding the free end across your chest, and the friction of the rope on your suit combined with the grip you have on the rope will stop me. Just one more term, Starn. What you're engaged in is the ancient and noble art of belaying. When you're holding me with the rope, I'm on belay, and when you're not, I'm off belay. You understand?"

"I understand," I said. "I just hope to hell that this rock wall understands."

"It will." And with that, he started up the rock. He moved slowly, but with a grace I had not seen before. He moved alongside a crack with a smooth rhythm, rising in short steps from resting place to resting place. I could hear his heavy breathing over the suit's radio, but that was all. He was silent as he climbed, and I realized that this was not the first time that Kelly had been on rock. Some of the fear eased back into the less conscious areas of my mind.

Kelly would stop occasionally and place a nut into a crack and clip the rope into it, and although he never looked down and I could not see his face through the reflected light of the helmet visor, I felt sure he was smiling.

At last he stopped. "Off belay," he said, and started to haul the beacon up towards him. The beacon bounced and swung going upward, but nothing short of a long drop would harm its rugged construction. "Haul line!" he called, and I dodged as the coils of the haul line dropped back toward me.

"Hook the tanks to the haul line," he said, "and then untie from the buggy and come on up. It'll take both of us to haul up the tanks."

I unclipped the rope and moved hesitantly toward the rock after hooking up the tanks to the haul line. There was nowhere to go but up, I thought, and stepped onto the rock, feeling the gravity pulling me downward. "I'm climbing, Kelly," I said.

"Belay on," came back from Kelly.

Kelly kept the rope tight as I climbed, crawled and panted up the rock. So far, it had not gone badly; and

I was beginning to believe we might actually make it to the top. I looked forward only to the next nut placement, where I could rest and regain my breath while I removed the nut and sling from the crack that Kelly had lodged it in, and then clip it onto one of the slings that Kelly had draped around me before he had started climbing. I finally crawled onto a small ledge where Kelly sat with the beacon beside him. He had anchored himself to another nut that he had placed deep into a crack at the rear of the ledge.

"Outstanding, Starn," he said to me as I collapsed beside him on the ledge. "Hell, I knew you could do it. That's one thing about climbing. You can't really tell anyone how to do it, it's just a natural ability that most people have forgotten they have. Let's get those air tanks up here."

With our combined efforts, we managed to drag the tanks up and on to the ledge. Then after a brief resting period, I clipped into the anchor and Kelly once more moved upward. We repeated the first sequence, what Kelly referred to as a pitch, and once more hauled the tanks up to where Kelly and the beacon sat. We were perhaps halfway up the wall then, and the height was becoming almost unbearable. I kept seeing myself falling, turning end over end to crash into the rocks below. I was sweating even with the cooling system of the suit on high. My fingers were beginning to ache from clenching small hand holds on the rock's surface, but nothing seemed to bother Kelly. Once again he moved up.

When he had anchored and pulled up the beacon, I moved off the ledge I had been belaying from. The sheer wall fell away below me to the ground. I couldn't see how Kelly had made progress and I told him so.

"Hell, Starn," he said, "There's a foothold around half a meter to your left that would hold an elephant. Move onto it."

"There's something there, all right," I answered. "But the damn thing's only about a centimeter wide."

And thus totally impossible to stand on, I thought.

As Kelly began to lose patience, his voice rose in volume and the small speakers inside the suit began to vibrate. "Damn it, Starn, there's enough rock there for you and me both to dance on. Now move on to it."

I tentatively stretched my left foot towards the flake. Touching it with my boot, I gradually shifted my weight onto my left leg and, surprisingly enough, the rock held me.

"Don't hug the damn rock, Starn. Lean back a little so you're standing straight up and down!" Kelly roared. "Remember, what's holding you onto the rock is gravity, so make it work for you, not against you."

It made sense all right, about gravity holding you onto the rock, but at that point, I was scared witless and all I could think about was what gravity was going to do to me when I connected with the horizontal surface far below. I was standing on a small flake with a crack immediately in front of me but no hand holds that I could make use of. "What now, Kelly?" I asked. "How do I climb this damn crack?"

"Use your jams," he replied cryptically.

"Use what?" I shouted back, wondering if I was supposed to be reading his mind again.

"A jam . . . oh, sorry about that . . . forgot you don't know how. Well, now listen. Take your hand, see, and make it flat and then insert it in the crack like a knife, O.K.?"

The sides of the crack scraped the knuckles of my gloved hand as I slid it toward the rear of the opening. "It's in the crack," I told Kelly.

"Good. Now turn your hand over sideways and then tighten your fingers and thumb into a fist. Make it big—make that fist grow till it squeezes tight against both sides of the crack and stays there."

"O.K.," I replied. "It's tight."

"Now lean back on that sonofabitch and feel it hold you there."

Kelly was right. I was secured to the crack by my

own hand, expanding to fill the dimensions of the crack.

"That's a hand jam, Starn. Another new term for you to remember. Now before that hand and wrist get all cramped up, take your foot and slide it into the crack sideways, with your knee bent outward."

"It's in," I said, my breath coming in short gasps.

"All right, now bring your knee and leg back toward vertical and your foot should rotate downward and jam tight against the sides of the crack. When it does, stand up on that foot and relax your hand. You'll be supporting yourself with your foot hold."

Again, Kelly was right and I slowly worked my way up the previously unclimbable crack using the jam techniques that Kelly had explained to me. My respect for Kelly and rock grew greater as Kelly would talk me up a difficult section, always with the rope tight against my middle in anticipation of a fall. I finally arrived slightly below where Kelly sat wedged into a large split in the wall. He sat with his butt firmly pressed against one side of the split while his knee and toe of his boot pressed against the opposite side. He was anchored to a nut he had placed in a smaller crack in the inside of the split. The beacon hung suspended from the nut, swaying gently below him. After I caught my breath, we slowly brought the air tanks up and tied them off to another nut placement to support the weight.

We were both breathing heavily, our suit tanks down to a quarter full. Off towards the east, Desolation's horizon darkened with a shifting of shadow. We had perhaps an hour left before lightside would slip from us like numb fingers from a small hold. I was beginning to appreciate why Kelly hated to climb in the dark.

He looked down at me from his position in the split. "This is called a chimney," he said. "The trick here is to use opposing pressure so you can maintain friction between both sides and some part of your body. Now watch me close, it's technique that counts."

He moved up the chimney with little effort, one foot and arm thrust in front of him, one foot and arm behind. Ten meters up, he suddenly stopped and cursed softly into the mike. "Can't protect the bastard, have to move out on to the face." He muttered more to himself than to me. "Why not," he continued, still talking to himself. ". . . there but for the grace of rock . . . O.K., Starn," louder, snapped like an order, "you'll come up the chimney, it'll be easier for you. I have to move out onto the face to get up. Be ready to hold a fall and remember there's nothing between me and you but bare rope, no running protection."

"Why the face, if the chimney is easier?" I asked.

"Easier for you, I said," he answered. "The moves are easier on the face but you might freeze up from the exposure." And with that, he deftly levered himself from the chimney onto the sheer vertical surface of the face. He moved with the rhythm of a spider, in quick short steps from hold to hold. The rope ran up and out, catching light like one thin spider strand of web, hooked to some crazy silvered arachnid that had lost four of its legs. For a moment, when his right foot slipped, he hung against the face awkwardly, boot moving slowly downward. Sweat instantly beaded from my palms onto the inner surface of my gloves and the breath caught in my throat. He was falling, but then, slow motion like, he leaned backwards away from the rock and his weight settled on to his remaining foot hold. He brought his right boot back to the hold it had slipped from like a wayward child that had to be coaxed. I could see he was near exhaustion but he didn't rest. He kept moving, upward. He disappeared over a rounded knob and remained out of sight as I waited to see his body suddenly appear spread-eagled and falling, feel the rope tighten and drag me from my fragile stance. A chill spread upward from my stomach, reaching for my heart. I knew we were dead, I knew. . . .

"Off belay and anchored." It roared in my ears. For

a moment I thought it was a scream, the sound a dying man makes when he falls.

"Dog damn it, Starn, I'm up. Are you still there or did you take a walk?"

A chuckle of relief started in my throat, but caught in my dry vocal cords and came out as a muffled cough. "Yeah, I'm still here," I said into the suit mike. "I thought maybe you were taking a nap up there or something."

"I just might do that when you get your butt up here," Kelly said. "Make sure the haul line's clear. I'm going to bring the beacon up the face."

I swung the beacon out of the chimney and watched it rise towards the sharp line of rock against space. It bumped over the edge and was gone.

"It's up," said Kelly, a note of relief in his voice. "Here comes the haul line."

I retrieved the loose end of the haul line and tied on the air tanks. "O.K., Kelly," I said, "they're secure. I'm climbing."

"Belay on, climb away."

I moved up the chimney imitating Kelly's earlier positions. My right hand and boot against the rock in front, my left against the rock behind, I crept upward, moving boot or hand only centimeters at a time. The technique worked fine, but I could feel the strength beginning to ease out of my muscles, and the weaker I felt, the harder I pushed against the rock. I suddenly realized why Kelly had moved out into the face. The rock sloped gently outward as it rose above me. If Kelly had slipped while in the chimney, he'd have fallen through clear space until impacting upon the stance I had been belaying from. If I slipped from the chimney, I knew the same would happen to me, and whether Kelly could hold my weight freely suspended from the rope was a question I didn't want to consider.

The muscles of my legs felt like weak rubber bands stretched to the breaking point. My foot slipped downward without warning, then my hand began to slide and I felt the rope tighten against my waist. "Kelly," I screamed, "I'm falling!"

"No you're not," he answered calmly, "you just think you are. The rope is tight so you're not going anywhere. I can hold you here all day but there's no way I can pull up your whole weight, so climb, damn it."

"I can't!" I screamed in terror. "The chimney narrows above me and I don't have room to keep my legs out." My foot had slipped completely out from behind me and I hung straight down with my face and chest against the rock. My boots no longer touched rock at all but were dangling in open space from the overhanging chimney. "What do I do, Kelly?" I whispered, waiting for the ground to come racing up to meet me.

"First thing is calm down. Now," he continued, speaking with a steady voice, "if your feet have slipped, get one back up under your butt and wedge your knee against the rock in front of you."

I tried to raise my leg up but was too close to the rock. "I can't."

"The hell you can't! Now listen to me—push yourself back from the rock with one hand till your back touches. Don't worry about falling, damn it, you're not going anywhere. After you do that, reach down and pull your leg up with your other hand if that's the only way it'll come, but get the damn thing up there."

He was crazy, I knew he was crazy, but somehow I managed to push backward, supported by only the rope that led upward to Kelly. I raised my leg up perpendicular with my body but the boot was just too heavy to move. I looked down and a wave of nausea hit me, but with my remaining strength, I reached for my ankle and jerked it up under my thigh and felt my boot touch the rock behind me and my knee brush the rock in front. "All right," I said, "I've done it."

"Good. Now I'll give you a little slack and you can rest for a minute."

"No!" I yelled. "Wait a—" The tension released from the rope. Instead of falling, my weight settled onto my leg, wedging my bootsole and knee tighter into the facing walls of the chimney.

"O.K.?"

"Yeah," I said, and pulled my other leg up beneath me to match the position of the first. I rested a few minutes until my breathing settled down to a low rush in my ears. My arms were still weak but no longer felt numb to the elbow.

"Well, are you ready?" said Kelly.

"Ready for what?" I replied tersely.

"To climb."

"I don't know if I can," I mumbled.

"Sure you can, Starn. Don't freeze up on me now."

The rope tightened and I pushed my body upward a few centimeters at a time until I had risen a full meter. With my feet wedged tight beneath me, I asked Kelly for some slack.

"What the hell for?" he said sharply.

"I gotta rest, Kelly," I said.

"The hell you do," he replied angrily. "You quit now and you'll stay there forever. Now climb!"

"Damn it, Kelly," I said. "I can't."

"The hell you can't!" he yelled, his voice rising in intensity. "You want slack, you got slack," and the rope coiled loosely around me, moving downward. "Now climb, you low-grav ground-pounding useless sonofabitch, climb!" he screamed. "I won't hold you any longer."

The lousy bastard would let me fall.

Anger boiled away my self-pity. He's trying to kill me, I thought, and my anger turned to rage and I knew that I somehow had to reach the top or he'd let me die on the rocks below. It no longer mattered that my legs ached and my arms were numb. I didn't care if I had to climb another thousand meters, I'd waste that bastard.

I struggled towards the top. Move one knee, then the foot. Push with the hands, the back . . . move the other foot. Slowly I edged towards the top of the overhanging chimney, oblivious to height, pain, rock. I finally dragged myself over the outward jutting crest and collapsed in the shallow crack that sloped gently upwards to the narrow, plateau-like summit of Horizon's End.

Gasping for breath, the rage slowly died within me and although the last part of the climb was a blur, I realized that there had never been more than a half-meter of slack in the rope the whole time I had climbed. Kelly's scheme had worked. I was up.

Kelly tied me off and then moved down to join me. We hauled the air bottles up and over the edge, then moved back up to the high point and set up the beacon, aligning it toward Deso Prime. With the beacon set and operational, we sank down onto hard rock and prepared to wait. Deso Prime would route a boat to us as soon as they locked on to the beacon's signal. In a few hours we would be relaxing back at the dome.

Kelly sat with his back propped against the beacon. "Well, Starn," he said, "We made it. You're a full fledged rock-rat, now." Those were the first words that Kelly had spoken since I reached the top.

"Ah, Kelly," I said, embarrassed at my performance. "Thanks for getting me up. I'm sorry I froze like that."

"That's all right," he answered. "It happens to the best of us. It happened to me the first time up so don't let it bother you." His voice was heavy with fatigue, the words slurring together.

I was drained of energy even though we were victorious. My suit stank of dried sweat and fear. The air through the filters was stale and heavy. A bit too stale, I realized, and checked the readout to find my tanks nearly empty.

"We better change tanks," I said, rising to my feet to retrieve the spares.

"Drag them over here and I'll switch for you," said Kelly, remaining in his seated position.

Changing your own tanks in the field is a minor problem, but it can be done. I was more than willing, however, to accept Kelly's offer and trade off on the chore. I pulled the tank packs over to where he sat and turned to squat in front of him so that he could reach the fittings. There was a soft hiss of escaping air as he snapped free the first tank. He latched the coupling of the replacement tank and then repeated the process with the second tank.

Desolation had grown darker while Kelly worked. The suit coolers murmured into silence as the heating units kicked in with a faint hum. I glanced over my shoulder and saw that darkside had swept up on us as Kelly had switched my tanks, the temperature starting to drop as residual heat began seeping from the planet's surface.

"O.K., Kid," Kelly said. "You're tight."

I turned in a half circle. With our helmets only a few centimeters apart, I could see through the reflective visor that masked Kelly's face. His features were drawn and the muscles of his jaw sagged from exhaustion, making him look older than he normally appeared.

"Turn around," I said, "and I'll do your lungs a favor."

Kelly slowly rose to his knees and turned away from me to expose his back, steadying himself with one hand on the beacon. His movements were awkward, as if he were dazed. The climb hadn't appeared to tire him at all before this, and I was a bit puzzled by his behavior.

"Kelly," I said.

"Yeah."

"Ah, never mind," I said hurriedly, at last realizing the obvious. Kelly had been in his suit before I had and had led the entire climb. Add to that the exertion of hauling up the tank packs and there could be only one result. His oxygen consumption had been greater than mine and his tanks were probably now near the danger level. I quit wasting time thinking and quickly twisted the fitting on his first tank and pulled, tossing it off to the side as it came loose. The replacement slid into place, another quick twist of the fitting secured it. I flipped the demand valve on and relaxed, knowing the air from the fresh tank would clear his head in a short time.

"Starn," said Kelly, after I had finished switching his second tank. "What was it you were going to ask me?"

"I was wondering about the beacon," I said, as I stood up and reached for the knobs on the transmitter.

"What about it?"

I leaned over and pretended to check the transmit dials. After I fiddled with the knobs a few seconds, I glanced down at Kelly, who was once again in a seated position, leaning against the beacon.

"I just thought that we might have trouble with it drifting this high up," I said.

"No problem, Starn. That rig is as solid as the rock we're on. They'll send a boat out for us shortly."

"Yeah, I guess you're right," I said, glad that Kelly had believed my answer. I didn't want to embarrass him by mentioning how low his tanks must have been. He must have forgotten to check his gauges in the excitement of reaching the top, yet it still seemed odd. One of the first things you learn when working dirt is to keep a close eye on your gear, and Kelly was a veteran of at least four other mining operations before he ever hit Desolation.

My thoughts were distracted by what sounded like the faint cracklings of a jump boat in my suit speakers, relayed through the receiver override of the beacon. I turned and looked toward Deso Prime, but the sky was empty. So much for wishful thinking.

The pressure of Kelly's gloved hand on my arm caught my attention. He waited for me to squat down beside before he said anything.

"Here," he said, placing something in my hand. "This is for luck. You've earned it."

It was the medal he had worn as long as I'd known him. He had taken it from the outside of his suit and I realized that he must have placed it there while still in the ship, unsure of how the climb would ultimately end. I turned it over in my palm and read the simple inscription: EVEREST EXPEDITION—2174—SOUTHWEST FACE. In the center was a raised likeness of what was unquestionably a large mountain.

I clutched the medal tightly in my fist. "Kelly, are you sure you want to . . ."

"Yeah," he said, answering my unspoken question. "I've never shown that to anyone out here. That's Everest, Starn, tallest piece of rock on the earth. She's a beauty, covered with snow and ice. You don't know what snow is, Starn, but it's white and it's cold. You'd be surprised how peaceful it can be."

He stopped speaking then and seemed to turn inward, perhaps thinking of old climbs and older rock. Far to the western horizon, the sweeping line of darkside's shadow overcame the falling sun, leaving Desolation's surface encased in soft greys. The momentary silence was suddenly interrupted as Kelly was overcome by a coughing spasm.

"Ah, Starn," he said, when he was able to catch his breath, "I hate like hell to say this, but I think I've got a problem."

A slow chill began to spread outward from the base of my neck. "What kind of problem, Kelly?"

"I think I've got a leak in my air supply."

"Jesus!"

"Yeah."

He hesitated for a moment, then looked up at me. "Maybe you better take a look at my tanks again," he said.

"Maybe your first set was running too low and it's taking a while to flush the system," I said hopefully.

"No way," he responded. "I always keep a close eye on my air supply, Starn. I was on reserve when you switched tanks, but nowhere near the danger point yet."

The chill continued down my spine, coming to rest in the pit of my stomach.

Once again, I found myself facing his back, staring at his tanks with growing apprehension.

"See if you can find something wrong back there. I can taste Desolation and I sure as hell don't like it."

I checked the tanks and fittings on his suit. They looked undamaged and seemed to be tight and in the right position when I gave them a light tug. Kelly and I both knew that a small leak would be hard to find without test gear and damn near impossible to patch up in the spot we were in. The chill in my stomach hardened into a tight knot of fear.

I quickly checked the helmet seat of his suit, looking for a small break. Nothing visible. He shifted his position slightly, becoming edgy at my silence. I briefly glanced at the rest of the suit, and then it suddenly hit me: "Patch up."

"Don't move," I said, and gingerly reached down and applied thumb pressure to the top edge of the plasti-foil strip that covered the rip in the right leg of his suit. Instead of adhering to the suit's surface, the material curled slightly under my thumb.

"It feels like there wasn't enough sealant on the surface before you stuck on the patch, but then the pressure test—you *did* run a pressure test, didn't you?"

"I was working on the air fittings while the damn patch was setting up, and then—"

"Damn it, Kelly, that's the kind of stunt a greenhorn pulls!"

Kelly sighed, then lapsed into another coughing fit. He started to speak and then stopped, as if he were unwilling to say what was on his mind. Finally, his voice rasping and low, he said, "I'll be damned if I'm sure what to do about it."

I searched my mind for possible ways of sealing the suit, discarding ideas as they surfaced one after the other. They all required a sealant, the basic fix-all we needed but didn't have. On the borders of awareness, a realization kept sliding through and around my other thoughts. As long as I had know him, this was the first time that Kelly had ever seemed uncertain of what to do.

In and among the logical ideas, I kept getting snagged on a memory from my childhood. When I was a kid, I'd had an eco-cube by my bed that I would watch for hours. It wasn't that much, just a small cube filled with water, some odd sea plants, and a few fluorescing fish from Bathard IV. The cube was self-contained and recycled the essentials. What fascinated me the most about the thing was that the gases the fish needed in the water would collect under a small shell on the bottom of the cube. The gas bubbles would finally lift the shell and stream to the top, the fish darting through the rising bubbles.

I kept seeing those bubbles lift the shell.

I kept thinking that this was a hell of a time to revert to my childhood.

My next thought was that the most obvious answers are the hardest to see.

"Kelly," I said, "I'll ease up the pressure in your suit."

"What the hell for?" he growled, sounding as though he thought that this time, I was the one going vac-happy. "The patch is already sprung, it'll just make the leak worse."

"No," I said, "We'll just make sure the leak is out, not in. Just don't move around much so you don't strain the patch more than you have to. You'll lose a little oxygen but it's a hell of a lot better than letting Desolation's atmosphere seep in."

Kelly always was stubborn. He thought about what I said before he would agree to up the pressurization. He started coughing again, badly, and it seemed to decide him.

"All right, Starn," he said, "We'll try it. I'll increase the pressure and see if it helps."

"Better let me do it with the override valve on the

tanks," I said.

"Why?" he said suspiciously.

"I don't think you can get it high enough with the in-suit control. We'd better balloon your suit just a slight bit to be sure of an outward leak."

"Damn it, Starn, that *will* blow the patch," he said.

"I'll take it up slow," I said, keeping my voice steady. "That way you can watch the patch and make sure it doesn't loosen any more than it already has."

I was still kneeling behind him, a few centimeters away from his back and I reached out and started to adjust the valve before he could say anything more. As the pressurization gradually increased, the suit began to bulge just slightly in shape.

"Starn," said Kelly, "Wait a . . ."

"Keep your eye on the patch," I said, cutting him off, as I gently increased the pressure.

"Ah, looks O.K. so far," he said. "That should be enough to do it."

I had to agree with him. His suit was still flexible, but ballooning enough to ensure the leak was outward. I kept my hand on the valve, grateful that he couldn't see my face. What Kelly needed in the worst way was a good dose of oxygen, not just simply to reverse the leak. His in-suit control was mainly for adjusting his oxygen supply to handle different work loads. The control was a safety device of sorts. It prevented the man inside from overpressurizing to the point that the suit lost flexibility and became a rigid trap. It could happen, but only an inexperienced man or a fool would let himself get caught that way. Men had died in ballooned suits.

Like I said, Kelly was stubborn. He would never have agreed if I had given him a choice. I shoved the valve up to max.

Kelly's suit expanded, straightening into an immobile orange star. He lay on his back, spreadeagled in the ballooning suit and stared up at me, his eyes burning through his visor into mine.

He said, softly, "You bastard." Then he was silent,

except when another coughing spell hit him. His face would go a bit pale then, but never his eyes.

The jump boat from the dome arrived a few hours later. It came in low and flat, slightly to the west of us, then seemed to pause and hover, and I quickly reset the valve on the back of Kelly's suit, bringing the pressurization down to normal before the boat slowly swung towards our location, landing arcs blazing a path of light through darkside's covering.

Stef and Dak both recovered from their injuries after treatment from the medicos back at the dome. Kelly's throat was sore and his breathing was ragged for a few days, but it cleared up. We'd been lucky enough to solve the suit problem before Deso's atmosphere had caused him any permanent damage. Our downed boat was air-lifted back to the dome and after a few weeks' work and refitting, she was out flying L and R's again, as sound as ever.

The crash had caused a lot of excitement at Deso Prime, but things finally quieted down and returned to normal the way they always do. The only difference I could see was that the climb Kelly and I had made was the favorite topic whenever we were swapping yarns with the rest of the guys.

We must have told the damn story a hundred times, always breaking up the listeners when we'd get to the part about Kelly being hoarse for a week after we got back to the dome from all the yelling he had to do while he was dragging me up the rock. I never mentioned the bad patch leak in Kelly's suit and neither did he. I couldn't see how it would add anything to the telling, so we just kind of forgot about it.

Kelly hung around until we started work on Desolation's second dome, then caught the first deep spacer through to God knows where. I never did know for sure why he left, but I suppose it was because Desolation was starting to grow. Kelly didn't like too many people around. I guess he went looking for more constants. I remember his last words to me, though, as if I'd just talked to him.

"You see, Starn, climbing is a dead art," he said. "No one remembers how to do it or has the time to learn, but what's important is, we beat the bastards, the ground pounders that say it can't be done. Remember that, Starn."

So like I said, maybe I'm a little crazy but I still like to go up to Horizon's End and watch darkside come on, and remember. I'm the only one left of the original crew still on Desolation. The others are dead or still mining out on worlds where there's no one to bother them. And I still fly jump boats—never did make it to rams, but then, I've got my hobbies to amuse me.

When Kelly left, he gave me a few of his holotapes, some of the only ones of their kind. They were old, and they explain climbing techniques, and I've tried to put them to use. That's how I came to run the school you are asking about. Kelly's High-Angle Ascents—climbing instruction and basic survival.

Look under: INSTRUCTION, SPORTS, in the directory. I'm listed.

A SECOND SOLUTION TO THE THIRD DR. MOREAU
(from page 79)

Answer 2:

If you divided 49 by 7 to get an answer of 7 hours, you score zero. One microbe becomes seven after the first hour. From there on, the sequence is the same as before. Therefore the container is 1/7 full after 49 − 1 = 48-hours.

Now for a third question. Suppose Dr. Moreau III put just *two* microbes in the empty container. After how many hours will it be *at least* 1/7 full? Answer on page 221.

THE AGONY OF DEFEAT
by Jack C. Haldeman II

We felt a few words about the illustrator of this series of strange sports stories might be of interest: Rich Sternbach lives in rural Connecticut with his wife, Asenath Hammond, two large tomcats, and an assortment of plants. He claims he is trying to raise triffids. He shares his garden with a family of woodchucks. After majoring in biology in college, Mr. Sternbach attended The Paier School of Art. His hobbies include gourmet cooking, modelmaking, and swimming with porpoises.

Albert Huff couldn't stand losers. Every player on his team knew that only too well. It was a fact for sure. Big Al ran the Castroville Artichokes with an iron hand and a terrible temper. He didn't get where he was by being Mr. Nice Guy, no indeed. Even the defensive line trembled when he walked by although each of them was three times as large as Al and strong as an ox.

Matter of fact, they *were* part ox.

Genetic engineering sure spiced up the game. It also made for a powerhouse team and their opponents, the Daytona Beach Armadillos, being mere robots, were running scared.

Big Al wanted this one. He wanted it bad.

It was billed as the game of the century. Of course every Superbowl was called the game of the century, but that didn't matter much. This was it—the *big* one, the whole ball of wax. Bulldog Turner Memorial Stadium was filled to overflowing, a sellout crowd. Scalpers got fifty bucks for crummy end zone seats. Anything near midfield was simply unobtainable at any price.

It was a glorious day for football.

Cashing in on some of the glory was the Hawk, interviewer *extraordinaire* and nosey s.o.b. *par excellence*. He was down on the field finishing his pregame show by throwing loaded questions at Bronco, the Armadillo's star quarterback. Bronco was a crackerjack passer and a third generation Mark IV robot, sports model. He was also a nice guy.

The Hawk wasn't.

"Tell me, Bronco, how does it feel to know that you're going to get clobbered by 800 pounds of pure muscle? The Artichokes led the league in quarterback sacks, you know."

"Well, Mr. Hawkline—"

"Just call me Hawk." He poked the mike closer to Bronco and turned a little so that his best side would be facing the camera.

"Well, Mr. Hawk, those are the risks, part of the game. But I wouldn't be honest if I didn't admit that I'm a little nervous. Nobody likes to get hurt, not even a robot."

"You mean you can feel pain?"

"Of course. I've got a program for it buried in my chest right next to the one I use for my shaving commercials. Robots hurt just like everyone else. I've seen my share of pain. I wouldn't be human if I hadn't."

"What about the scandals?" pressed the Hawk. "The illegal will-to-win circuits?"

Bronco blushed. He had a program for that, too.

"If you don't mind, Mr. Hawk, I'd rather not get into that." Poor Gipley Feedback. His heart had been in the right place even if his head hadn't. He was doing five to ten at the state prison. Poor guy had tampered with the system in order to restore the glory of football and now he was paying the price. Bronco hoped they'd let him watch the game.

"I'll bet you wouldn't," said the Hawk. "But the public has a right to know and we'll get to the bottom of this even if—"

"Up to your old tricks, eh Hawk?" It was Big Al, cutting across the field with Moog and Quark, halfbacks for the Artichokes. Not only were the two players part ox, but they were part gazelle, too. They looked funny, but they sure could run.

"What's this I hear about you selling your team by the pound if they lose today?" countered the Hawk.

"Your nose is out of joint, Hawk."

The Hawk's nose was a sore point with him, being of the wooden variety. His natural-born nose had been bitten off by an Arcturian. It hadn't exactly been the Hawk's finest moment, but it had saved the day for Earth.

Big Al was one of the few who could get Hawk's goat.

"Would you like to explain to our viewers, Mr. Huff, how you think you can get away by playing with a genetically engineered squad when the rules clearly state that football is too dangerous to be played by humans?"

"Come on, Hawk, get off it. You know as well as I do that these guys ain't hardly human. Wouldn't take a court to figure that out. How 'bout it, Moog, you human?"

"Irg."

"Quark? How 'bout you?"

"Mug mug."

"See?" said Big Al. "Dumb as rocks. Added together they couldn't scrape up 12 points on an IQ test, not even on a good day. They may not be smart, but they can play football."

"But—" A tuba knocked the Hawk flat on his back. The band was coming on the field from the sidelines. A clarinet stepped on his hand.

"That's the latest from down here," he said, getting to his feet and trying to make his way through the percussion section. "Now back to the booth and Roger Trent." He stepped on an armadillo. Seemed to be thousands of them on the field.

There were only a couple hundred, actually.

From the opening kickoff it was obvious that the Armadillos were in trouble, big trouble. The Artichoke's front line was as tough as a brick wall and just as impenetrable. It was rumored that they were part cinderblock, but that had never been proven.

It was 21 to 3 when the second quarter opened. Castroville was threatening to run away with the game.

Roger Trent sat in the broadcast booth with the Hawk, shaking his head. He was an Armadillo rooter from way back and it didn't look like it was going to be his day. He suspected the Hawk would like to see both teams lose.

As humans go, Roger was old, really old. He had been a superstar for the Baltimore Colts back in the days when flesh and blood people were still allowed to play the game. He kept trim and youthful because he had a lot of money, more than enough for rejuvenation treatments. The money came from a film based on a book he had written about his days as the last human quarterback in a field being taken over by robots. The book was called *Hell's Alley* and it was about football, but when the movie finally came out it had a different title and was full of monsters.

"Second and five. Bronco takes the ball and hands off to Woods." Roger Trent called the plays and the

Hawk provided the color and irritating remarks. "He tries to find a hole up the middle and is smothered by a pile of Artichokes."

"Gonna be a bad day for Woods," said the Hawk. "He averaged 4.37 yards a carry for the year but he won't be able to get near that today. That line is tough. They wouldn't let their own mothers through."

Their mothers were test tubes, thought Trent, but he didn't say it out loud because it might get the Hawk mad. He wanted all the best lines for himself. Best lines were probably part of the Hawk's contract.

"Third and long," he said instead. "Bronco's going back for the bomb. He's trapped. He's down."

The Hawk had missed the play. He had his nose in a thick book.

"Woods is a third year veteran with the Armadillos. Prior to that, he played two years with the Key West Jellyfish."

"They're going into punt formation. Devin gets a good one away, taken on the ten by Garth for Castroville."

"During the off season, Woods sells insurance and plays flamenco guitar at an Italian restaurant."

". . . brings it out to the thirty before he's brought down."

"Who was that?" asked the Hawk, looking up from his book.

"Garth," sighed Trent.

"Seventh in the league in punt returns last year," said the Hawk, leafing quickly through the book. "Averaged 32.73 yards per return. Garth is ten percent cheetah. You can tell by his whiskers and the way he growls when the ball is snapped. In his career he has run seven punts back for touchdowns, although two were called back when the films showed he had bitten a potential tackler. Only last year against Philadelphia, as I recombulate my memory, he . . ."

The Hawk talked through three straight plays. He did that a lot.

"I like your nose," said Trent in exasperation.

"Sit on it, Roger."

The Hawk was hitting his stride.

Unfortunately, the Armadillos weren't hitting theirs. By the half they were down by two touchdowns. It was only by frantic heroics that the point spread wasn't more than that. They were getting clobbered.

The halftime show was a double barreled extravaganza, even bigger and better than last year's double barreled extravaganza. It was dutifully ignored by the spectators who spent the time crowding around beer stands and jamming into rest rooms. The players spent the halftime getting patched up and reprogrammed for the second half. The Hawk spent the halftime trying unsuccessfully to sneak into the dressing rooms. He had to be satisfied by interviewing a man dressed in an artichoke costume who was about to dive from a fifty foot ladder into eighteen inches of melted lemon butter. The dive was a success, but the interview was a flop. The Hawk liked his artichokes with Hollandaise sauce, not lemon butter, and his prejudice showed.

The second half unrolled like a carbon copy of the first. Casualties mounted for the Armadillos as they tried to bring down the mighty Artichokes. Woods went out of the game with a dislocated circuit board. Bounds was on the bench with every fuse in his chest blown. Pope's arm kept falling off.

In their huddles, the Artichokes congratulated themselves, patting each other on the back and picking small bugs from their partner's mangy pelts. They had everything under control and they knew it. They hooted a lot.

Only with extreme effort did the Armadillos manage to keep the margin of defeat down to two touchdowns. They were playing their hearts out, just managing to hang on. It was a pitiful sight as one by one they were hauled off the field on stretchers, tears welling up in their optical scanning devices. They wanted to win this one, win it for the memory of dear old Gipley. It would take a miracle.

The miracle got a nudge just as the two minute warning was flashed. Someone unlocked the cage that held the Daytona Beach mascots. Two hundred armadillos scuttled onto the field. It was in the middle of a play and confused things a lot. The Castroville Artichokes, not being very bright, mistook the armadillos for loose footballs and pounced on them. Taking advantage of the chaos, Bronco tossed a long bomb to Tucker in the end zone. The Artichokes protested, but there was nothing in the rule books against armadillos on the playing field. Castroville tried to get revenge by rolling artichokes around at the line of scrimmage, but nobody would confuse an artichoke with a football, not even a robot. The kick was good and Daytona Beach trailed by seven points. But with a minute and a half left in the game, all Castroville had to do was take the kickoff and sit on it, letting the clock run out.

Devin's kick was deep and taken in the end zone by Glunk for Castroville. He elected to run it out in order to use up more time. It was a mistake. Heading towards him with murder in his electronic eye was Wild Bill. As dedicated as any robot on the squad, Wild Bill had fury in his plutonium heart. He wanted the ball. They collided on the twenty with a crunch heard all the way to Rockville.

Glunk went down, hard. Wild Bill disintegrated in a shower of cogs and levers. The ball was loose, bouncing end over end There was a frantic scramble for the ball, but when the dust cleared it was Rusty who came up with the pigskin for Daytona Beach. The crowd went wild. The Armadillos had been four touchdown underdogs. Too bad there wasn't enough left of Wild Bill to share in the excitement. He had given his all.

Two plays later, Bronco ran the ball across the end zone on a perfectly executed quarterback sneak just as the final gun sounded. All that remained was the kick for the extra point. But Bronco was worried. That would just tie the game and they'd have to go into a sudden death overtime. Castroville had never lost a sudden death. They'd be murder. They might even block the kick. As they went into the huddle he decided it was all or nothing. They'd go for the two point conversion.

"They're lining up in kicking formation," said Roger Trent from the booth. "The ball is snapped. Wait! It's a fake. They're going for two. Bronco has the ball, he's moving fast. It's a reverse. No, a *double* reverse. He's going back to pass. *Look at that!* The old Statue of Liberty play. Carter takes the ball from Bronco. He's going around the left side of the line. The Artichokes seem confused."

"*I'm* confused," said the Hawk.

"He's in! They've done it. The Daytona Beach Armadillos have snatched victory from the jaws of defeat."

"The Statue of Liberty play went out with spats," grumped the Hawk.

Bronco was flat on his back. He'd been hit hard. With tremendous effort he raised himself up far enough to look over the three sides of beef that had clobbered him to see Carter go in for the big one. He smiled. Victory was sweet.

Big Al was furious. He flattened his quarterback with one punch. The loss would cost him his job. He beat his tailback silly. He kicked the bench over.

The Hawk was down on the field, trying to grab an interview. The only person he could get close to was Big Al. Everyone with any sense at all was staying well away from him.

"Well, Huff," said the Hawk, jamming a microphone into Big Al's nose. "How does the bitter taste of defeat go down?"

Big Al took one look at the Hawk and there was nothing but raging fury in his eyes. He bit off one of the Hawk's ears. The left one.

Not again, thought the Hawk. *Why me?*

Big Al's mind had snapped at last.

"Not bad," he said, chewing away.

"Could use a little lemon butter," he added, loyal to the end.

THE FAR KING
by Richard Wilson

The author, for the past 14 years the Director of the Syracuse University News Bureau, and before that, editor with various news services, learned his trade as a military historian with the Army Air Corps in the South Pacific during WW II. His story, "Mother to the World," was given the Nebula award for best novelette by the Science Fiction Writers of America in 1968.

It was ironic that Ann Bagley got mixed up with a bunch of extraterrestrials in a night club at the top of the Mile-Hi Building in Chicago. But maybe it was inevitable. She was the daughter of the minister of a flock in a place like Zion, Illinois, home of the ecclesiastical fig newton, only it was a smaller place. I won't name it here, or name him. Ann Bagley or, as she was later called, NoNo McCanless, is not her real name.

I'll call him the Rev. Ezekiel Bagley. His sect is one of many that interpret the Bible literally. But his own interpretation includes the belief that there are alien lands that have been touched by the hand of God. He used the concept once in a sermon and it evoked such a response that he kept it in and soon built his gospel around it. He is pastor of the Church of the Rediscovered God of Earth and Undiscovered Lands Beyond, as he renamed it.

His children, three girls, were born in sin, he believed, because the Book had it so and therefore he was as harsh with them as he was with his wife and himself. He lived an austere and humorless life as he strove, with limited wisdom, to make the world a better place by denouncing its pleasures. Only in this way, he was convinced, could there be salvation in another world.

He never said in his sermons, or to his family, where that other and better world might be or how to get to it. He read books he'd bought second hand or ordered cheap by mail. He had shelves of works that mixed fundamentalist dogma with far-out philosophies that took his fancy or provided a peg for a sermon. He was not above lifting other people's stuff, knowing it would go unrecognized by his congregation of simple folk. Sometimes he preached a weird one:

"Think not that you are the only ones chosen of God. We on Earth are mere dust motes in the sunshine of his far-flung radiance. Many there are on other worlds on whom His mercy shines. These aliens—alien to us, not to Him—may please Him more than we do. In fact I think it likely that we sinful creatures find least favor in His eyes. Do you doubt? Then let me share with you, my fellow sinners, the discovery by a learned man who proved that at least three other planets within our reach have intelligent life. Mathematically one of these could harbor God-fearing creatures with intelligence vastly greater than ours. Is this not, my brethren, a humbling thought?"

And so on. He'd quote from his latest second-hand book and hold it aloft. He'd give his flock glimpses of pertinent passages underlined in red.

"Go and repent, my brethren, and pray forgiveness, and seek salvation through Christ Jesus whom we must recognize as but One of a number of Sons of God doing His work throughout the cosmos."

Her father's sermons had a somber effect on the daughter who was to be NoNo McCanless. Their impact was greater because she'd gone to his study and had read for herself the underlined passages and the paragraphs around them. He hadn't made anything up. It hadn't been revealed to him in a supernatural way. Other people were saying the same things and these things were published in books. She'd always had respect for books.

Maybe this is what planted in her young mind the belief that one day she'd travel to a far world and meet the living savior. Christ was dead on Earth, or at least gone from it, but maybe on a sister planet His Brother lived and walked among men, unfettered by limitations of space and time. Maybe on that other world He was mortal yet and she'd find Him. And He'd—He'd— It was too fantastic a thought to pursue—who could fathom the mysteries?

She tingled in her teenage way and daydreamed. What would Jesus's Brother's name be? He'd be a Stepbrother, of course, but His title would also be Christ, which meant King. Her own father had said it was possible. His books said so. She might meet

Him, one day, if there were a way to get there. Or He might come here in His magical way, for surely the Divine Brothers would be in communication and would visit Each Other. Exalted, she went to bed and dreamed of her Far King.

§ § §

I knew her then as a down-the-block neighbor in a village with no secrets. Her father preached to a small but full house each Sunday noon. His words thundered out to his little multitude. I was unwillingly among them, between my parents, and I knew the effect of the words on them.

I didn't know then where he'd got the words. His daughter Ann was to show me. At a church supper, urged by her mother who knew mine, she asked me to help serve the apple cobbler. We took ours to a table at the far end of the basement kitchen. She called me by name. Everybody knew everybody else in the village but we hadn't formally met.

"I really admire your father," I said. "I used to hate church before he came." I politely bent the truth.

She ate daintily, half as fast as I. She put down her fork and chewed and swallowed before she replied. "He has a lot of books in his study. Would you like to see them?"

I said I would and she took me there. "He reads all the time," she said. "Mama says 'Come to bed' and he says 'In a minute' and he keeps reading and making notes. Once I got up in the night because—excuse me—I had a cold and Mama'd been feeding me juices and I had to go to the bathroom and he was still up, reading and writing. I asked him what he was doing and he said 'One day you'll know, my child.' "

I took a slim green volume from a high shelf. I was intrigued by its title, *The Far Kingdom*. She said: "I've looked at that, too. It's underlined a lot." We were fourteen or fifteen then.

§ § §

I went back often, at his invitation, relayed by her.

I wasn't allowed to borrow the books but I could consult them there. At first I read out of curiosity but the more I read the less strange they became. Each was persuasive in its own way but one often contradicted another. I began to see what Ezekiel Bagley had done. They weren't *his* books—he hadn't written them—yet they were peculiarly his because of the way he'd annotated and crossbred them. He'd made a careful selection of the theories of their authors about extraterrestrial life and God's role in it. He'd built a working synthesis that he preached to his flock. Perhaps it was significant that a boy and a girl should have been caught up in this mass of words.

Once when I was engrossed in the green volume or one like it, Ann, sitting close beside me, read to herself from the Old Testament. I supposed she was going back to the accepted text to seek better evidence for her dream of a Far King. She was reading the Song of Solomon and had come to one of the parts that describe the body of the Shulamite maiden: "Thy two breasts are like two young roes that are twins." She read it aloud to me, then said: "I wonder if mine are. I never thought about it." She unbuttoned her blouse to look for herself. Young girls didn't wear brassieres in those days, at least not in the Bagley family, nor was she wearing a slip.

I must have gasped when she exposed her young breasts and regarded them with new interest. "Do you think mine are like roes?" she asked, moving so I could see better. "Young roes are fawns, you know."

I stared, unable to speak, then turned away.

"No; look and tell me," she said. "Breasts aren't bad or they wouldn't be in the Bible."

I looked again, knowing my face had gone red.

"Well, are they?"

"I don't know," I said finally. "I thought it said, uh, breasts like pomegranates." She shook her head. "But I know where you mean: 'As a piece of pomegranate are thy temples within thy locks.' Solomon also says 'Thy plants are an orchard of pomegranates' and that must mean another place. I'm only talking about breasts. Do you think mine are like twin roes?"

"How does the Bible mean that?" I asked. "Their shape, or—"

"He also says in Chapter 7 'Thy stature is like to a palm tree, and thy breasts to clusters of grapes.' "

"Your—yours are more like grapes, I guess."

She cupped them one at a time, then with both palms. "I guess so. They're hard and soft both. What do you think?"

It seemed to be an invitation and I reached out a hand. She took it and drew it toward her.

There were footsteps at the end of the hall. Without haste she let go my hand, rebuttoned her blouse and turned the pages from Solomon's Song to Revelation. Her father opened the door and came in. He nodded. "Nothing I like more than to see young people reading Scripture together," he said.

"We wanted to know if another Jesus is mentioned in the Bible," she said, cool as could be.

Her father gave us a little sermon on original sources and the Apocrypha/Lost Books of the Bible but I don't remember much about it. I can't even remember whether I touched her breast or, if I did, whether it was like a cluster of grapes.

We were youth-pure then, still to taste the world. Had I not left the village we might have met often, talked and truly touched and loved, married and raised typical children in a typical small town. But I left and she and I did not meet again until many years later in the 5280 Club in Chicago's Loop.

I'm Jack Norkus and I come into the story here and there, now and then.

§ § §

I'd spent many years in the Mile-Hi Building, a day visitor among aliens from worlds unknown to our space explorers, when Ann Bagley came in one cold night. I scarcely remembered her as she stood at the door, cold from the wind and wet with snow, seeking shelter denied her by the YW, overbooked that New

Year's Eve.

"What made you come here?" I asked.

She was looking around the 5280 Club in amazement, as well she might. It was not yet the dawn of interplanetary, let alone extrasolar, commerce as far as she and most of the other people of Earth knew.

Boots the bartender welcomed her in his transuniversal way and said "What will be yours?" and I led her to a far booth, away from the stranger residents.

"I knew you'd gone to Chicago and I needed somewhere to stay," she said. "What is this place, anyway? Some kind of circus—theater?"

I explained that most of them had arrived at one time or another on the Midnight Shipment. They were traders, businesspeople, scholars. For starters, I introduced her to a few of them—they slithered, rolled, oozed, or floated over to the table. She met Mogle, who's a triped; Diskie, who disappears when sideways; JorenzO the Black Magician; and Lopi of All-Planets Films. She was polite to them and they to her; she was taking it well for a person who had expected to spend that night at the YW. She also met Dan and Joe and Keith and Frank, Sam and Moe and Leif and Hank: a handful of Earthlings who, like me, had gained entreé by accident or because the aliens needed them in their commerce and gave them guest privileges.

I don't want to go into a long explanation of how people from a dozen worlds speak the languages of the others. They don't. Some of us can hardly speak our own. If anybody cares, there's an operating manual on the linguapathophone in the message center that's run by Dan McQuarrie, a graduate student in linguistics who commutes from South Bend twice a week. He's a serious young man with a B.Sc. from Glasgow University. If you let him he'll talk you numb about linguapathic telecommunication, for which the Mile-Hi Building is wired in its upper stories. It's a kind of voluntary bugging. Everybody wears a skin-colored plug behind his ear, or whatever he has that gathers sound waves. Not everybody has skin, either, but the device adapts. One of the alien traders—it was Luo of Ulo—had brought its forerunner with him and sold Boots the Chicago concession. It's since been refined; it no longer weighs six pounds. Luo weighs 2,370 pounds, so don't let him step on your foot. Before that, I'm told (I hadn't explored the Mile-Hi Building then, though I lived in its shadow), communication was by sign language or pointie-talkie or other primitive means.

Things are simpler now. For instance, when Eosho wants to trade Daemonian dream capsules for ropes of red licorice, the linguapathophone puts the whole transaction in crosscultural socioeconomic terms, simultaneously computing the current rate of exchange.

Thus if I buy a rope of Chicago licorice for two cents and Eosho's dream capsule costs him the equivalent of a nickel, we trade at five of mine for two of his and we are satisfied. I don't know what he gets for red licorice on Daemonia but I bet it's a bundle. I can get up to twenty bucks on the street for one of his dream pills. It beats delivering pizza, which is what I was doing when I discovered that the Mile-Hi Building was not entirely empty above the tenth floor, as most people supposed in those New Depression years.

The Mile-Hi Building rises like a gleaming needle implanted in the lime-rind of earth. It was built by a visionary architect named Fallon and became known as Fallon's Folly when the New Depression hit and the building failed to attract tenants above the tenth floor. The upper stories were closed off to cut maintenance costs and no one knew that aliens had taken over at the mile-high level.

Then, by means of the Midnight Shipment, the top several stories filled with alien beings who used the upper quarters for offices, trade, and recreation. Mayor Daley's successors never knew there were extraterrestrials among them, trading with Earthmen without the sanction of the Chicagoland Industrial Board, trafficking in strange goods without the knowledge of the Chamber of Commerce, helping the economy of Earth and other places without the imprimatur of the Metropolitan Development Council.

In somewhat the same way that the linguapathophone works, the various reconstituted alien atmospheres are blended into a mutually acceptable mixture that, when I first noticed it, was faintly pink and smelled agreeably of Christmas tree tinsel burning on the third rail of a toy electric train track. Now I'm not aware of it any more.

Somewhere once I'd seen a directory that listed the tenants of the higher stories. I don't remember whether it was in the upper building itself or at the base of that yawning vertical cavern which joins the inhabited areas. The shaft, designed by Fallon to carry a high-speed freight elevator, had been converted by the aliens to house an antigrav platform activated by a bypass button known only to the aliens and those they trusted to use it discreetly. It was the most frightening thing in the world when I first had to use it, delivering pizza from the mundane world below, but now I find it as routine as riding an escalator. Except for JorenzO the Black Magician and a few others, the aliens don't use it. They make contact with the surface of Earth in other ways.

The directory has since disappeared. As I recall, it looked something like this:

All-Planets Films; Lopi, Producer-Director	528-4
Archives & Library; Skwp, Scribe	528-7
Club; Boots, Manager	528-1
Combined Earth Intelligence	528-19
JorenzO the Black Magician	528-13
Laurel-Eye, Madam	527-2
Midnight Shipment	529
Mogle; Agent	528-6
Society for Prevention of Space Travel	528-18
Zichl, A.; Imported Spirits	527-1

I wasn't sure how factual the board was. Was it significant the Society for Prevention of Space Travel adjoined Combined Earth Intelligence? Were either or both a joke?—or a cover for another kind of operation? I'd heard that Diskie was a double agent for Earth and the Extrasolar Consortium, whatever that was.

Anyhow everybody talks his own particular patois and everybody else understands him. Not always perfectly, of course. Dan McQuarrie goes on about that if you let him; he's full of shop talk and linguistic anecdotes. Sometimes he gets excited and lapses into gutter Glasgowegian; he was lowly born, like most of us. That's when I tune out his clear speech and listen to him through the bug. Then everything is plain.

So that's why NoNo McCanless, as Ann Bagley came to be known, and the future Far King, when she finally found him, were able to talk each other's language. Literally, that is. As it happened there were basic misunderstandings on each side. Even when we're culturally close, ambiguities befall us. In NoNo's case nobody, least of all NoNo, blamed them on the linguapathophone.

§ § §

NoNo McCanless had become a regular in the 5280 Club long before the arrival of the Far King, then Leo Reo, heir apparent to the throne of Farland. Probably she's seen as much of hard times as the rest of us terrestrials since she left home, as I had earlier, to seek her way in a world beyond the confines of that narrow village. I could sympathize with her ambition, which I supposed was to make a good marriage, not necessarily a romantic one, with a man who'd provide for her comfortably, with whom she could be compatible and beget a child or two for immortality's sake. As I say, I could sympathize with that. But it was hard for me to accept the way she passed the time among us while she waited for her prince to come.

Over the years I've seen a few women in the 5280

Club, all of them Earthwomen except Laurel-Eye, the alien madam who sometimes relaxed there away from her duties in her own establishment a floor below. The visitors to the club are women such as are found in any bar and, because the club has its own special way of being exclusive, most of them are normal adventurous women who offer more than their bodies and brighten our existence with wit and charm and their special viewpoints on life. That's the kind NoNo seemed to be. She was lively and had a skill. She worked in clay, making figurines of the characters who drifted in—up from the Loop or down from the Midnight Shipment. She made witty effigies of Diskie and Boots and Mogle and Don McQuarrie and me. She always made two and fired them up and presented one to her subject. A thoughtful thing to do.

But later she grew morose. She spent a lot of time in the far booth that had become hers and read a lot in books, sometimes marking the pages as her father had done years ago.

But sometimes she'd rouse herself into an antic state. Oh, we all knew NoNo. We knew her somewhat; not well. She rebuffed familiarities that were more than superficial. She'd drink your liquor and eat your meals and give you bright, witty conversation. She'd kiss you if the mood was on her but it had to be her kind of mood—the hell with yours. She'd run into you somewhere in Chicagoland and you'd have a drink and drift over to her place and neck for a while but in a cool way, interspersed with high-minded conversation. The next day you'd be practically strangers again.

Sometimes at the club she'd fling herself into our laps, if we were Earthmen, and we kissed her and hugged her and laughed and danced energetic dances with her and perspired a lot. But her kisses were quick, biting, tongue-darting—no warmth or duration. And nobody, really, sat and talked to NoNo McCanless. Not meaningfully, intimately. It wasn't only into human laps that NoNo flung herself when she was in her hyperactive state and the spirit of seeming abandon was upon her. It may be that she learned from her father that all creatures, from whatever world, were God's creatures. She was as apt to arouse an alien by ruffling its rufa or tantalizing its tertiary talon as she was to tease a terrestrial in the way we all knew and, in our frustrated enjoyment, deplored. (   ) the inscrutable said once out of his experience with her: "If she biffles my iffle one more time I'll wurble her what into a permanent plerm." Knowing the powers of (   ), it was an awesome threat.

I knew how he felt. After one such exhibition when NoNo seemed to be teasing me more than any other in that mad group before abandoning us all, in my frustration I visited a sperm bank on North Clark Street. It was a place where customers for my Daemonian dream pills sometimes hung out. None was there this night and I required rent-beer-food money, so I gave of myself. Some give free at such emporiums because the means of extraction is so interesting. I went only for the money, I told myself.

Later, NoNo was more skilled at fending off males. It was still important to her to be liked and she was likable up to a point—a point she defined in her own way.

JorenzO the Black Magician, who reads minds, listened one night as we discussed NoNo in her absence. "She's a mystery woman," Don McQuarrie said. "Why try to explain her?"

"I can explain her," JorenzO said in his pompous way. "I have studied her psyche and know why she is as she is. Will you hear?"

We protested that trespassing on her mind was repugnant to us, that we really didn't want to hear. No, no, we said; then yes, yes.

He began. He told us theatrically, weaving mind images that made us reluctant but fascinated voyeurs. It was as if we were portraits on a wall that looked down on all that had happened to her.

NoNo, then Ann Bagley, had once married. She'd wed a weak man who'd threatened suicide if she wouldn't have him; it was clear that he intended to go through with the threat. But then, married, there were no children, though both said they wanted them. It was her fault, he claimed; all his ancestors had had children right away, mostly male. Obviously he thought male was better. He taunted her in company, despite tests that had shown them both fertile, telling anyone who'd listen: "I'm all right. If only I had a real woman." Knowing it was no more her fault than his, unable to be with him after that, she left him. But, knowing that she could conceive and wanting not to, except with her chosen man, she fended off all others. Not only did she never let a man get close to being physically amorous, she allowed for fallibility or accident by using every possible precaution as it came along: the pessary, the pill, the coil.

And when the demand came, as it sometimes did when her other creative ways failed her, she'd fling herself among whoever was present and laugh and sing, and twist and shout but not give out, and achieve a kind of release to tide herself over to a new day when she might read a book and mark it, or sculpt a likeness, or write in her notebook. Or sit and wait for her prince.

NoNo came in as JorenzO finished his oral dissection of her. She went to her far booth. JorenzO disappeared in his magical way. Boots set up a drink for her, on the house. She thanked him and looked around. We raised our glasses to her. Poor NoNo! She was dear to us that night.

§ § §

NoNo's notebooks were private, she thought. She didn't know about Boots's attenuated pseudolenses which could snake across the room more invisible than spiders' strands to see what she wrote.

She didn't know about the talents of Diskie, a

two-dimensional Slivian. Diskie looks like an oversized coin under a foot in diameter. Because he has no third dimension he's weightless and can hover at any level. And because of his lack of substance he can go through things or beings, or stay inside them. When he's not on end he's shimmery, like a silver dollar with a big face on the obverse that changes at his whim from terrestrial to extrasolar. On the reverse of his coinlike body appear and disappear mottos in English, which is the *bêche de mer* of the upper reaches of the Mile-Hi Building: Thin is Beautiful, Tomorrow the Whorl, Absorbed by Another, or The Inside Story. Diskie wasn't born or hatched, he said, he was minted; and when he entered NoNo it was in an asexual way. Thus he too was able to help flesh out the story I might have called Inside NoNo McCanless.

Nor was NoNo aware of the extraordinary ability of Skwp the alien scribe to receive, file and retrieve anything verbal from anywhere.

According to my youth-learned standards none of them should have spied on NoNo and later on her and Leo Reo, nor should they have let me or anyone else see or hear the transcriptions. But because my standards have withered I can summarize a selection from NoNo's supposedly private journal and tell about things that happened later.

Listen to NoNo, writing in the third person and supposedly only to herself:

Nobody knows you when you're old and gray, they say, and she wanted none of that. If an occasional strand of gray marred the glory of one so young she'd pluck it out; if there were many tell-tale strands she'd dye them and their neighbors. Once she'd let it all go back to natural and had been aghast at what had happened in so short a time. Actually it had been a number of years—five? six?—but she'd stopped counting.

One's youth flits away the timelessness of the early years. For a while it's springtime and summer but all too soon the leaves have turned. The future becomes less vast, less limitless than it was. The years, once ever-extending, become finite and countable. A person wonders for the first time how long she's got. Is there time to do all she wants to do? If there's a chance that there is, hadn't she better get started? Hadn't she better activate the dreams, influence the future, delay the drift? Isn't it time to steer the no longer everlasting now toward a foreseeable future?

One thinks about this abstractly at first, then more demandingly as the seasons change—especially if one is no longer a girl but a woman addressed by strangers as ma'am.

One's dreams of the future, once so pleasant, become nightmares of anxiety. Once it had been all so possible, so put-offable, because one was so young, so full of promise; but now youth was running out, her promise only a perhaps.

A kind of panic set in for her. All the time in the world had dissolved into a disturbing fear that the once-bright future had shortened, clouded over. This was a sad situation for a woman of fewer than 40 years. It resulted in her flinging herself into life as she thought it should be lived. It was a panic reaction that need not have been, if she'd settled for less. But NoNo had vowed to settle for no less than the best. Some day her Prince would come. Of that she was certain. Some day he would ride to her from wherever he'd been to wherever she was. He would be radiant and she would glow and there'd be electricity in the meeting, thunder and lightning, a sound like temple bells, a throbbing in the psyche, and all the other manifestations of a meeting ordained.

§ § §

It happened almost that way with the arrival of Leo Reo, the future king of Farland.

There were alien snicks and clackings when one of us of Earth talked about the fine figure Leo Reo, the future Far King, cut as he favored the Mile-Hi Building with his presence. The total of this twittering in alien tongues—not that all of them have tongues—was that they knew better. Chances were slight that one from another world could be so like a human being as the visitor was. The impression was that his shape was one he'd assumed for the purpose of his voyage.

There was speculation about that purpose. Not even Skwp, the alien scribe, was yet able to give us hard facts about Farland. It was a place too recently known to have been programmed into his data bank.

Laurel-Eye contributed to the scuttlebutt. She said she'd heard from a customer that the Farlanders were so new that they were still experimenting eugenically to learn what shape they should be to adapt to their adopted land. Not only was their agriculture in flux, with their farmers seeking the best alien corn, but the species itself awaited improved hybridization. The new planet had been artificially cooled to a habitable state and was facing problems that arose from accelerated evolution. The best breed of cattle and other food animals had not been stabilized; and the people themselves were in a transitory state, still seeking the optimum means of copulation for maximum growth of population. So much for Laurel-Eye's contribution.

Lopi of All-Planets Films claimed Leo Reo was Lopi's own creation. Lopi said he'd been canning a quickie on Quintus V some millenia ago and had hired an itinerant for a supporting role. If that hadn't been Leo Reo, or maybe his great-grandsire, Lopi said, he'd ingest his intaglios. But who can believe a showman?

(   ), our disembodied voice, said he knew a Far King from long ago as a perennial wanderer under an intergalactic curse who leapt from planet to planet as often as was necessary to flee his Nemesis, breaking hearts along the way. (   ), the inscrutable, who was something of a moralist, said he recalled an incident on Taurus 20 where the being called the farking—the words joined and lowercased—had found A, a trisexualite; and B, an assenting amoralist; and that C had ensued, with long-range effects on the local proprieties. (   )'s stories tend to get diffuse and I put this in for the record.

Diskie told of a far place in a time past. He had been whirling invisibly sideways, to avoid being obliviated, when a corporeal creature very like Leo materialized and spoke in a prophetic way, causing consternation among the populace. Leo forthwith became a God for Whom to this day Faraway-Long-Agos set out hollow burls of warmed kvish which they ceremonially inhale. Zichl purveys a similar product but most of us prefer Boots's brew.

The universal drink in the 5280 Club is beer, but not the bloating, carbonated product that passes for the working man's beverage on Earth. Boots's beer is an alien elixir, cheap, satisfying, mind-sharpening. Boots brews it from an ancient formula, and it's what we need to warm ourselves in the evening of a trying day as we relax and let our minds roam free, comfortably open to pleasing thoughts and to companionship in this haven high above Earth's problems.

Boots has other potions behind his bar and will dispense them on demand but his beer is the best and far cheaper.

Some say it is less an intoxicant than a tension-easing drug, concocted to keep peace in the club, an antidote to or substitute for hard liquor, pot, and whichever mysticism you found helpful.

Whatever it is, we like it, and like its price.

Mogle was the most skeptical about the royal lineage of Leo Reo, potential Far King. "If he's a prince," Mogle said, "I'm an octopus." But Mogle *is* a sort of octupus.

§ § §

JorenzO said: "I've seen him before, gallivanting around the safer planets, enjoying the local pleasures. Sure he's a prince—his daddy rules a kingdom the size of Winnetka. Some day, if he lasts, he may be the two-bit king of a minor world."

"You have to admit he cuts a good figure," Boots said. Like all bartenders, he was a diplomat. "Leo lends class to the joint."

"Only because he squinches a lot and leems," said ( ), inscrutably.

"Here he comes," Boots said. "He usually buys for the house. Anybody who objects to that can withdraw." Nobody withdrew and all drank Leo's health in their refilled glasses, myself included.

"A pleasure to see you all in such amity," Leo Reo said, letting his eyes roam to the far booth. NoNo McCanless was absent from it.

Leo Reo's first stop on Earth was the Mile-Hi Building, and he never got beyond it. As a matter of fact, having debarked from the Midnight Shipment, he went no lower than the 528th floor. Of all the aliens who'd traveled to Earth this inhabitant of Farland was the only one with a completely terrestrial look. None of the others could pass for very long. JorenzO the Black Magician did at times but he practiced his deception from a stage and never mingled with the audience.

Each saw Leo Reo as he or she (NoNo) expected to see him. The aliens in the 528 club found his nonhuman shape as acceptable as any of their own. They also knew how he appeared to terrestrials and would not consider disclosing his secret.

It was part of the code of the interstellar trader: protect your buddy against the outsider. No matter that we of Earth considered ourselves the insiders; to them the top of the Mile-Hi was no Earthly holding but an alien enclave. So NoNo and I and all others of

Earth saw not the reality but what he projected to our minds—a princely being of pleasing Earthly shape. The illusion must have been all the more titillating to them later as they observed certain goings-on between NoNo and Leo Reo in the far booth. The secret of the prince of Farland was safe. Even Boots, NoNo's friend, held his tongue, or whatever he did in his idiom. He might disapprove of the alien's actions but he'd not betray them.

Some have said cynically that if it hadn't been for Leo's royal lineage NoNo wouldn't have given him the time of day, except to sit in his lap and kiss him in her brief and darting way and twist and shout but not give out.

As it happened, he made the first advance. NoNo had come in, looking neither right nor left, and had gone straight to her far booth and read a book with yellow marking pencil in hand. The book was a compendium of the great thoughts of man. She had marked Blaise Pascal's Pensée No. 355:

"Princes and kings sometimes play. They are not always on their thrones. They weary there. Grandeur must be abandoned to be appreciated. Continuity in everything is unpleasant. Cold is agreeable, that we may get warm. . . . "

Leo sent NoNo a drink. She sent back a note: "Join me." He did and I ached to listen. Others eavesdropped and I knew later what was said. I reproduced the essence, skipping the dull parts:

Leo: "We haven't met."

NoNo: "A pity. Rectifiable. NoNo McCanless."

Leo: "Leo Reo. Enchanted."

NoNo: "You don't look enchanted. You look ordinary. *Nice* and ordinary."

Leo: "I'm just a guy. You keep yourself marvelously well. You must be happy."

NoNo: "Happy is relative. Are you?"

Leo: "Mostly. I am a royal relative. There are gaps; surely you know."

NoNo: "I know sadness. I know nothing."

Leo: "A conundrum? What do you read?"

NoNo: "Like Hamlet, words."

Leo: "I know his words. I read thoughts. Shall I read yours?"

NoNo: "If you dare."

Leo: "Your thoughts are chaotic, inchoate. You have the body supreme but ask whether your mind is its equal. You have dreams that reality denies. You know there is more than you have known so far. Am I wrong?"

NoNo: "You are astute. Are you more than clever? Are you the one I've waited for?"

Leo: "I am myself, here, now, and we have met by chance. Often I distrust chance but not tonight. Do I sound like everyone else? It serves me right."

NoNo: "It serves you well. I have waited for years, it seems, filling in the hours, not diluting myself. I read, I learn, but years pass. Once I was seventeen and all that it meant. Now I'm wiser but I deteriorate."

Leo: "You must have been magnificent to have deteriorated to your present perfection."

NoNo: ". . . Shall I sit in your lap?"

Leo: "Do. Hurry."

NoNo: "You advise haste?"

[At this point NoNo McCanless closed her book, drained her drink and moved to his side of the booth. She put a leg across his lap and an arm on his shoulder. Back to the edited transcript.

Leo: "Cozy. NoNo? You are badly named."

NoNo: "I am mistress of my fate. You smell good, Leo, if that is who you are. You content me."

Leo: "I am myself. You see we have an audience. But if I placed my hand so who, from afar, would notice?"

NoNo: "None. I notice, though, and I am moved. Are you moved, Leo? Are you the one I've waited for? Are you the king of beasts?"

Leo: "Are you the queen of breasts?"

§ § §

I tell you, the eavesdroppers could hardly contain themselves. Would NoNo McCanless succumb? Would the heir apparent commit himself to a liaison? Were we watching a game? Who would win? Could there be a winner?

Leo Reo spoke again: "Shall we go?"

A pause by NoNo. Then: "Not to my place, nor to your place here. But to your place in Farland. The way it must be."

A pause by him. An equivocation? He spoke finally: "Are you content to wait?"

Her pause was brief. She spoke eagerly. Too eagerly? "No but yes. Yes."

"Then I'll wait, too. I'll try to send for you. Would you come?"

"Yes. Yes. I'll come."

There was no mistaking their language. His question had been in the conditional. Her answer was in the future positive. If it was a game he'd won. NoNo could not have known it then.

§ § §

Skwp the alien scribe—the "w" in his name pronounced oo as in "own"—looked like a department store mannikin seated behind a desk on rollers. It was hard to say whether the desk was attached to him or whether he was the desk. Whatever the combination, it was functional. There was the oval work surface bounded by print-out screens. Built-in data boxes lit when summoned and talked when spoken to. There were transmitters and receivers and filers and retrievers; and Skwp had, or was, all of them. He was a repository of facts. He was strongest on extrasolar statistics but skimpy about Earth. He'd tell you why: Terrestrial data were readily available. If you needed to know who'd won the fifth at Belmont on a certain Saturday, or wanted a list of unsuccessful vice presidential candidates, you could have it at the flick of a switch from Data Central-USA or from Combined Info-UN. Or find it in an almanac. For a Karloff filmography, a Beiderbecke discography, that kind of thing, you wouldn't go to Skwp. But if you were after the day's prices on the wodible market at Blech or the latest scores from the Tertiary Griads in Esteddis, O.D.K., Skwp could supply them at the touch of a mandible. His three mandibles snaked over the top of his desk or wandered around under it. His head was androidal. He had it made for him when he'd been assigned to Earth. His facial expressions were conventionally human, simulating smiles, frowns, thought, and joy, But they were far from convincing.

Skwp—may I call him Scoop from now on?—can I call him he?—was an agreeable fellow but his responses to terrestrial ways were limited. Once I showed him a frame from a film that had been banned in Des Plaines, Illinois, though hardly anybody anywhere was banning anything any more. Scoop caressed a series of stops that produced a read-out that read "Whoo-whoo!" He disappointed me. Of course he'd ingested the frame into his info banks and that was the important thing for him. I'd have been more pleased if he'd chuckled indulgently and told me about the complicated copulatory activities of the trisexuals of Taurus 20, as (   ) had done.

But I needn't apologize for Scoop's lack of humor. I was grateful for the information he'd gathered, on short notice and despite communication difficulties, on Leo Reo in his own far land and what had made him the way he was. For my benefit Scoop described Leo's background in terrestrial terms, to help me understand an alien ambience that didn't translate well.

§ § §

When Leo Reo was a younger man he was not the heir to the throne. He had an older brother who was hale and handsome, lean and learned, virile (having already sired sons and daughters) and valiant. Everyone knew the brother would be king one day and Leo's fate as son secundus was to preside over a principality far from the seat of power. So no one paid much attention to him, not even his father and mother. His father the king had him in to hear his lessons or to bestow on him a leftover family honor not worthy of the first born. His mother the queen saw him more often. She measured him periodically for height and weight and gave him ancestral trinkets from her side of the family. She told him of ancient glories and kissed him a lot in a dutiful way. They were close for brief lengths of time, but there were weeks when they were apart.

Longing for companionship, Leo found a friend. His father had an adviser on interpersonal relations who was many years younger than the king and not so many years older than Leo. His name was Neel and Leo came to adore him. He liked the way Neel looked (tall, lean), the way he smelled (spicy, inviting), the way he dressed (flamboyantly, with hidden rustlings), and the way he spoke to the young prince (intimately, excluding all others).

It was inevitable that they should become lovers. Neel's will and Leo's lack of direction made it happen. Even as it happened Leo wondered if it were a

princely thing to do. Occasionally, as he pondered the possibility of his elder brother dying, he questioned if it were kingly. Because of the lack of issue from this kind of relationship and because he knew that if he pursued it he might lose the ability, or the will, to know women in a productive way, he was disturbed and confused about his duties to the crown.

But his friend and lover (and adviser to the king) told him it didn't matter: in the rare chance that he survived his brother into majesty they'd work it out. It was the transfer of semen that mattered for progeniture, not the physical or amatory contact with the other sex. Their science had ways to preserve and transfer it, warm and pulsing still, to the wombs of waiting women. A detail.

So Leo's friend persuaded him to fully enjoy their secret life, knowing that, if Leo's brother died, he'd still be capable of siring princes and a potential king.

There was of course more than the physical in their association. There was a meeting of minds the like of which the young prince had never known. It was possible, with Neel, to speak of anything. Sometimes, interlocked in odd ways, they discussed art and poetry, architecture, and music. They sang together or composed verses.

"But you must live in the other world as well," the teacher told his protègé. "You must learn to simulate and dissemble." And so Neel taught him how to be charming to people of all kinds, including those of the other sex. Leo learned to stimulate women mentally and lead them subconsciously to desire him physically.

Such was the teaching that when his brother died in a sporting accident and, after appropriate mourning, he went out into society as the heir apparent, a countess and two princesses fell in love with him purely because of his conversation. He squired them impartially. Such was his success as a dashing and romantic public figure that one day his father summoned him. He congratulated Leo on his popularity but urged him to moderate his activities lest he give the impression that his father the king was ill or impaired.

Leo gladly curtailed his social life, as if in fealty to his father, and again took up his private life with Neel. Neel began to groom him for kingship, amid their pleasures, devising ways to assure continuity of the throne without the need to take a queen.

§ § §

Forward in time to the Mile-Hi Building. Inside NoNo McCanless, via Diskie and Scoop:

I was content today. My friend Leo Reo left a note which said: "I am not far, but am elsewhere than with you, which pains me."

I spent the evening in my booth and worked on two figures. One is of him. One looks like the me as I would want him to see me. I gave them to Boots, who put them on a shelf behind the bar and bought me a drink, two drinks; three drinks. He likes me. Does Leo Reo?

Now that I look again at the figures, the one I made of me looks a little bit pregnant. I didn't consciously make her that way.

§ § §

Scoop delivered the fateful message.

Leo had been squiring NoNo in his charming way for nearly a week. According to the eavesdroppers, there had been a hottening up of the atmosphere in the far booth of the 5280 Club. He, Leo, was interested in her and she, NoNo, was absorbed in their companionship. They had not gone much beyond conversation but their hands and knees had touched, their minds had met, confidences had been exchanged, and there had been tentative exploration of a number of possibilities.

Again, however, there was ambiguity in the language, despite the efficiency of the linguapathophone. Leo spoke in certain tones which the eavesdropping aliens recognized as laden with reservations, and NoNo spoke in a feminine hyperbole whose nuances men forever misinterpret. It appeared that each had for the other an attraction unmatched in previous encounters, although the guard of each was up. To Leo, NoNo seemed to be offering herself as his latest far-flung conquest, with the aim of making his list and boasting of it afterwards. The atmosphere was torrid, electric; the players cool. But I feared that his cool, compared to hers, was that of an iceberg to an ice cube.

I'm getting to the part where Scoop rolled in on his self-contained desk and delivered the message. Boots saw him first. He set up a drink and asked for a preview.

"It requires public dissemination," Scoop said, and toggled for amplification. The message, as Anglicized, boomed out of Scoop for all to hear, NoNo included:

"Hear! All concerned, pay heed. Hear! Leo Reo, heir apparent, my duty commands me say that your honored father, Potent VII, has chosen sleep as preferable to continued but impaired existence. The Council of Regents orders you to most expeditiously return and receive the sceptre of the late king. You will be known, in direct descent, as Potent VIII. Reply immediately."

Leo Reo, suddenly the Far King, stood to attention. He replied: "I return at once, on the Midnight Shipment. I, Potent VIII, the Far King, hear and, for the last time, obey."

NoNo listened to the Far King's words with quickening heartbeat. She must have hoped for a mention of herself (a queen so soon?) but there was none. But surely he had it in mind and she looked at him with confident eyes when he turned to her in the booth.

"Goodbye, my dear," he said. "As you heard, I am commanded to go. Be assured that if ever you reach my land you will have a most royal welcome."

NoNo chose to read into his words more than was there. "I hear you, O Prince, O King." I think she had drunk too much and he resented it on the occasion of his elevation. She went on: "I hear your call and I shall come, as soon as I am able. But, Leo, why not now? Surely—"

All of us heard him put her off with explanations of the solemn ritual and the preordained, inflexible rites. So she said she understood. She kissed him and let him go to prepare for his journey. She ordered another drink. She took out clay and went to work on two new statues. They were like the ones she'd done before, of him and her, only this time they wore crowns and the female figure was definitely pregnant. She gave them to Boots who put them behind the bar with the others.

§ § §

Leo Reo, the potential Far King, had been gone several months by our reckoning. No one could say with certainty whether his time was our time but certainly it passed with excruciating anxiety for NoNo.

Then one night she floated into the 5280 Club waving under our noses, or whatever we had, a validated ticket on the Midnight Shipment. "My king calls and I, his subject and future queen, must obey," she said. "I will send postcards, if postcards there be. You will always be in my thoughts. Now, Boots my friend, farewell drinks for all on me until the loading gong rings."

We drank her health and fortune and pretended to rejoice with her about the arrival of the ticket. The pretense was necessary because Scoop had already told us she'd bought it herself. There'd been no communication of any kind from the Far King.

There was a lot of scurrying around topside when the Midnight Shipment was due. It wasn't every midnight, of course; Earth didn't merit more than one or two transfers a month. Some of us suspected that when Leo Reo, a minor monarch, went to take up his royal duties on Farland no special embarkation had been arranged; more likely Scoop had delayed the fateful message to coincide with a scheduled shipment.

Outsiders were excluded from the sky deck when the Shipment was due. Insider-outsiders like myself were expected to keep out of the way and mind our business. Yet we couldn't help seeing cargo spew out of offices to be levitated to the deck. At the same time extrasolar cargo was offloaded and disappeared into the offices or storage spaces reserved by the resident aliens. Things and people came and went. NoNo went. I'd missed her more before. Neither of us wept.

§ § §

For a long time there was no communication with Farland. Scoop said that was to be expected from civilizations that had not stabilized themselves. Not to mention communication priorities when a hundred worlds tried to get through simultaneously, convinced that their trivia was as vital as official communiques.

But eventually there was a bleep—a mere peep—that Scoop fixed on intently because it was addressed to Boots. It was from NoNo. It said, in its entirety: "Bootsie: No one here makes a cocktail the way you do. Keep up the good work and save one for me. NoNo (YesYes)." Boots concocted one on the spot and put it at the back of the freezer, labeled NN/YY.

Scoop sent his circuits searching for another transmission and found this, which is what NoNo McCanless wrote to her former classmates at Carrie Chapman Catt College, for publication in the alumnae magazine, *Sisters Rising*:

"Greetings, sisters, from a far land called Farland. My message: Don't come unless you're officially invited and are well-connected. I came insufficiently prepared, having forgotten my Girl Scout training. I was taken in, you might say; I expected more than I got, having assumed a contract. I was misled, having chosen to believe I would be the first among women, which I am not by far. This humbles me, too late for rectification. You can learn from me, though. Heed what I say. . . ."

NoNo's message, which she sent under her real name, Ann Bagley, went on for a thousand words or more. Scoop reported that the editor of *Sisters Rising*, a contemporary in her thirties, found it incomprehensible and spiked it.

From NoNo to All Those at the 5280 Club, delivered by the Midnight Shipment, on the back of a triveofax showing a fuchsia landscape dotted with avocado umbrella trees under a rare triple sunset:

"It's better where you are. At least it's familiar. Who yearns for an alien shore? I, once. No more. Hey, Jack, 'I shall return.' Warm my booth."

§ § §

Let me, Jack Norkus, say in an aside what my father once told me, back when I first knew NoNo. He said Norkus was a corruption or simplification of the name for a four corners in England where his father and their ancestors had always lived. There were two such intersections in the high land they saw from their village. The nearest was the North Cross. I was reminded of a story about a man called Snooks who'd been jilted by a social-climbing woman who decided she could not live with the name. But then he was accepted by a more imaginative woman who gradually changed Snooks to Senoks and finally to the lordly Sevenoaks. "So," my father told me, "if you ever need it, know that you are not only a Norkus, which has been good enough for many generations, but also a Northcrosse. I hope you won't need it, but you should know it."

I guess he was saying we're as good as they are, whoever they are.

§ § §

Next from NoNo was a poignant transmission, she not knowing it had been scanned and, in a freak of atmospherics, transmitted from Farland to the cosmos, including the 5280 Club, via Scoop, for our edification, or voyeurism. It was probably lifted from her notebooks after she made the most of the few moments her royal friend gave her for old time's sake. Thus poor NoNo out there with nothing to relate to except him and his indifference, giving her a small part of the time of his day, squeezing her into his schedule out of kindness or guilt. Listen to her, if you can stand it:

We'd sit and talk sometimes, in an Earthstyle nightclub he'd reconstructed to assuage my homesickness. He'd say "Sit in my lap, you gorgeous sex object" and I'd get all fired up and cuddle close to him, gradually wriggling on to his lap, tousling his hair and seeking subtle erogenous zones like his lower lip, to nibble, or his collar bone, to run my fingers along.

This was exciting to me, with him. I'd done it so often with others, firing them up and then ducking out on them. I guess what it had achieved for me was a kind of orgasmic experience which didn't require going off with one particular man and all the complications and letdowns that would have involved. Forever free, that was me, flitting from one to another, using them for my gratification as long as they interested me, without delivering myself. It was grand while it lasted, though I don't know why they put up with it. It lasted until I met Leo Reo and emigrated at his behest. (Had he really asked me?) I'd come from Earth for him but had he really wanted me? The real me? As it turned out, no. All that mattered to him was the future of his race. I, there unbidden, but one of a number of catalysts that helped create the atmosphere he required before he bedded down.

His other helps, I learned, were exotic perfumes, potions and philtres of an aphrodisiac nature, erotic films, and certain organic foods. He used me and the other catalysts to assure the success of his repopulation plan. After he'd aroused me he'd say something like "Well, it's

time for beddy-by" or "Got to catch up on my beauty sleep" or "Can't keep the programmer waiting." And he'd dismiss me!

My handmaidens would appear as he excused himself to go to his unisexual six-poster, leaving me to get through the night as best I could. Some of my handmaidens had ideas about that, I could tell, from the way they anointed me, singly or in pairs, vigorously, daringly, giving me substitute pleasures for those I'd wanted with him. I never succumbed to their enticements, not so they knew, though I was tempted several times by their expertise and their insinuating ways. What always put me off was their smirking. I wasn't going to wind up as one of them, or give in to their voluptuous invitations. I treated them all as hired masseuses as I masked, while enjoying, the responses their skills evoked.

I'm through with him now, I guess. I have some residual feelings. I much admire the shape of his nostrils and the full curve of his lower lip. I value the conversations we'd had.

I'd like my child, if male, if there could be a child, to resemble him. If I permitted it to happen, knowing I could mold the new male in my way, not his, to Earth ways, not Farland's. . . .

It's up to me, of course. He's supremely indifferent. He's used me, as I've used others, and I don't like it.

But if there were to be a child it would be mine, not his, and maybe it would have the qualities I admire in him and none of his faults. Maybe it would have my good qualities, my talents.

He or she, my son or daughter, the poor bastard, could be the potential president, the someday scientist, the nouveau novelist, the future filmmaker, the artist supreme—or, in my poor deluded father's vision, the future Intergalactic Savior, spreading the gospel according to the

An angry NoNo, at a later time writing in her notebooks about her former adored, the Far King, Potent VIII:

He's about as potent as the bum who sells his dirty blood for a bill at a blood bank on North State Street. Not only didn't he know where anything was, he didn't care. He didn't have to know. It was done for him. Maybe that's the way of royalty—his kind of alien royalty—but it's not what he'd led me to expect.

His idea of a good sexual experience was to lock himself into his royal computing center and get his technicians to program a world premiere wet dream. Oh, he made a fine kingly ceremony of it but basically it was as romantic as the village idiot wandering around, hand in pocket, pulling his pud.

There he was, my former hero, in his ermine pajamas or the Farland equivalent, supine in his six-poster bed, alone in its sybaritic vastness, with electrodes at temples and gonads, the harness positioned to catch his climactic emission, oblivious to everything but his programmed pleasure.

What a waste of royal beefcake, I thought. But of course nothing was wasted. The technicians, hovering dutifully on the outskirts of his dream, saw to that. His precious seed was saved for sowing far and wide. Instead of having his philoprogenitive fluid wastefully trapped in a solitary female who might or might not conceive, the fellatioid machine ensured that every conceivable iota was preserved, frozen, banked. Later at intervals his input, as I've no doubt they call it in their antiseptic jargon, was thawed and distributed with impartial beneficence to unremarried widows, to unmarriage-

able maidens, and to wives of impotents. Any leftover stuff, restored to throbbing warmth, was introduced into culture dishes with pulsating, waiting-to-be fertilized eggs taken at their prime from maidens at the height of their nubility.

Nothing was wasted on Farland. Certainly not at the royal level. One component met the other, generation gaps notwithstanding, and lo! in time there was a child, and another and another, ad infinitum. Many turned out well. I've seen hundreds of products of matings past. They're strong, intelligent, handsome, and—it would seem—virile.

I have the making of such a child. It's with me always, chilled inside a capsule in an insulated locket between my warm breasts. Any doctor who has kept up with the abstracts can open the locket and make me the mother of a prince or princess.

One day, maybe. I'm young yet, I tell myself. One day, when I can forget my dreams of royalty and accept reality, I'll have a master carpenter build a six-poster bed and commission technicians to attach me to electrodes. Right now I'd mind terribly. O Leo Reo, what have you become?

But one day, when the pain has dulled, as it must, I'll take out the special tape he sent me with the locket and pretend I'm again with the king of Farland.

I won't have to pretend very hard—if I make up my mind to it and accept the indignity of the programming it can be very like the real thing. There'll be quasi-connubial bliss with the essence of the Far King in the wedding bed of my design. I'll be the uncrowned queen, along with a thousand or two others whose bastard children are entitled to wear his bar sinister. If I want it. If I succumb.

Would you accept me then, Earthman? Would

you have me if I came back riding a half-alien child on my hip? If you would, my friend, I'd no longer need to sit alone in a far booth and brood. Maybe once in a while you'd take me up to watch the midnight Shipment come in from lands beyond. Maybe then I'd belong somewhere.

This is Jack Norkus again. Or John Northcrosse, whoever the hell I am, speaking to you in Earth tones. Or as Earth-toned as one can speak in the Mile-Hi Building. Was NoNo talking to me, Earthman Jack, in the spied-upon entry in her private journal?

Would I accept her? Would she accept me without first taking to her mockup six-poster and having her electrodal, computerized coupling with her absent but real enough dream king—and then having her locket opened by a doctor or a competent technician to impregnate her with the real seed of the Far King?

Noble as he is, and impersonal as the method might be, I don't think I'd want to be the stepfather of his farthest-flung child

§ § §

They could have managed a better homecoming for her. Maybe it should have been up to me as her friend on Earth but I couldn't get enthusiastic about arranging a celebration for the woman who had jilted me—though she probably never considered that I might have been courting her. Possibly my feelings had never been expressed, had been mostly in my mind.

Anyhow, I regretted that no one had made a special effort to welcome her back. I'd almost forgotten that most of the people at the 5280 Club are aliens and that their ways differ from ours and each other's. To them she was one of hundreds or a thousand transients who make their way among worlds.

So when the Midnight Shipment deposited her and

she debarked among the handful of passengers and the multifarious cargo, she was cleared with impersonal inefficiency, just like everyone else. She surrendered her voyage papers, paid the mooring fee, made her mark on the roster, and went to the slide to seek her luggage. She had trouble finding it among the jumble and miasma of other creatures' belongings. She saw me then and gave a wan smile as she gestured helplessly. I went to help her sort through the alien mound and, alas, I believe I said by way of greeting, "How many pieces do you have?"

"Three," she said. "I should have carried them. Hello, Jack. How are you?"

Her words almost tore my heart out but there was little time for talk. She spied a bag and went for it among the jostling nonterrestrial passengers who muttered, "Surbis, surbis," as they made their way in and out of the mass. Something seemed to have her mark on it and, when she nodded, I grabbed it from under what looked like a five hundred pound mottled egg about to hatch. She saw the third, finally; and we withdrew to the 5280 Club.

"Shall we sit a moment?" I asked, not knowing her plans; and she nodded. I saw her eyes go to the far booth. It was occupied by a creature of fluid shape that also filled all four seats and the space beneath the table.

"I shouldn't have expected them to save my place," she said. We looked for another.

But then Boots came from behind the bar and, lightly touching her on the shoulder, said to the off-white creature in the booth, "Surbis, sir; reserved," (for our benefit) and chittered away in another tongue until the occupant undulated in a revolting obloid way to a table atop which it repositioned itself, assuming a shape like a giant pulsating haggis with a central sheep's eye that blinked in an offended way. Boots took the creature's drink, bubbling in an oversized egg cup, from the far booth and set it atop an unoccupied corner of the haggis's table. He suctioned clean the seats and table of the far booth, and ushered us there with professional ceremony.

As we sat opposite each other and thanked him he said, "The usual, I presume, miss?" and gave me a shrug that meant I'd get a beer.

"Beautiful Boots," she said and arranged her bags on the seat beside her. "It's good to be home."

"It's good to see you back," I said automatically. Our conversation died until the drinks came.

Then JorenzO the Black Magician stopped by in his stage regalia and said, "Have I got an act for you!" and proposed a carnival tour to exhibit the only woman of this world who'd been to another. She would lecture on her personal experiences, using holograms which Lopi could supply from his All-Planets library of exotica and erotica, faking NoNo into the picture. She thanked him politely; and he backed away, saying he'd draw up an itinerary, an outline of the act, and a tentative contract.

She and I had little time to talk amid the callers. It was a satisfying welcome after all. Even A. Zichl, the imported spirits person, who'd always been stingy with his expensive trade product, came by. He delighted us with an OmniOmelet, made of eggs of five planets and seasoning of six others, and a small unlabeled decanter of a mellow brew.

So maybe it was better that each of us welcomed her in his own way and that instead of a big formalized hello there were lots of little ones.

§ § §

Relaxed and sleepy but with no place to go, she was granted a special dispensation by her alien friends and given one of the club's guest rooms for a couple of nights. I understood from them without being told that I could have shared it or used a connecting one, if that was what she and I wanted. Wordlessly she and I decided otherwise and I went to my place outside. I carried on what trade I could in the streets during the day and visited the club nights.

She was different now, this person who had gone away and returned. She was calm, more thoughtful, and often seemed lost in reverie as she sat once again in her booth. I didn't intrude. She'd look up and nod when I came into the club but didn't invite me to join her. She read, or wrote in a notebook or did her sculpture. Once or twice she shuddered as if in the grip of an unpleasant thought and put up her hand to feel through her blouse as if to be sure the locket was still there. She drank rarely now and in the days that grew into weeks after her return she did not become antic or wild.

She was again a regular in the club but not a mingler.

I learned what she was writing in her journal—a handbook with the title "Alien Sex Customs: A Guide for Earth Women."

She still answered to NoNo or Miss McCanless but she had a new name, according to the byline under the title. The name was Nina Queen.

§ § §

NoNo and I had said little to each other since her return and I was even less inclined to seek her out after my discovery that she was using, if only privately, the pen name Nina Queen. Probably it was merely merchandizing, to help her sell the book. Nevertheless I felt that her royal pseudonym reflected a continuing fantasy, a delusion that she still might one day meet a Far King, of the kind her father had preached so persuasively. I thought: NoNo the Ice Queen, retreating from human contact within a fortress of frost.

And did she not still wear between her breasts—were they warm now?—that damned locket of his chilled sperm? It had become an unconscious gesture of hers to touch it through her clothing, to caress it lightly, as her eyes looked far beyond any of us.

Damn those breasts and those eyes and that symbol of potential consummation! Damn NoNo and the effect she was having on me still, despite my growing conviction that I should forget her and find someone uncontaminated by aliens, not warped by the preachings of a father obsessed by visions that had come not from his God but from readings in crackpot tracts. I should quit this sick outpost of space and its gallery of sideshow specimens and look for peace beyond the shadow and memories of the Mile-Hi Building. It should be possible to find someone like Kipling's "neater, sweeter maiden in a cleaner, greener land." Somewhere such a maiden must exist for me, if I had the sense to seek her. Somewhere away from the Ice Maiden, the absurdly but aptly named NoNo McCanless, lost and lonely and undoubtedly brave but rapidly becoming a character to be pointed out to tourists.

I went, saying goodbye to no one, but went perhaps not as far as I should have. I found a lake in a neighboring state where I rented a cabin and a rowboat. It was early spring. I bundled up and rowed, watching the season change and the green appear in that clean land.

I went to the village library and looked through books, wondering where in Kipling's poetry I'd read of that sweet maiden. I didn't expect to find her in "Mandalay." In among all the rousing thunder and exotic sounds of the East as voiced by a Tommy shipped home to gritty, drizzly London. Hidden in the next-to-last stanza, imbedded like a jewel, it is one of the few lines in the entire poem not distorted by a Cockney accent: "I've a neater, sweeter maiden in a cleaner, greener land!"

I went back to Chicago, to that silver needle stuck in the green rind of an Earth fruit not yet ripe enough to welcome the aliens living among but aloof from them in its mile-high eye.

I went back with nothing resolved, my plans no clearer, not knowing whether I'd speak to NoNo or she to me. It just seemed to me that I was going home to a big city's special neighborhood that had accepted both NoNo and me.

They asked where I'd been, said they'd been looking for me, there was a message from Leo Reo.

"For me? Why me?" As far as I knew, the Far King hadn't communicated with any of us since he left. The message was a Scoop Special, a facsimile of the ornate scroll in which the original must have left the royal palace of Farland. It said:

My dear chap—

First permit me to congratulate you on the happy news. I regret that I will be unable to be present at the nuptials but my fond wishes go to you both. There will be a suitable gift at the proper time for you and your fiancée. I am not writing separately to Ann, for reasons that you and I as men of the world can appreciate. As one of your proverbs has it, "Once smitten, too often bitten."

This then is solely for your eyes . . .

I looked up. Boots, JorenzO and Scoop were pointedly paying no attention to me. I knew damn well every one of them, and any number of others, knew what Leo had written. They were at the bar, a discreet distance away. NoNo was not in the club.

. . . and I leave it to your excellent judgment how much of it, if any, you will wish to communicate to Ann.

Here is what I must tell you—you may consider it another wedding present or you may curse me:

The locket which Ann Bagley, alias NoNo McCanless, wears between her sweet breasts carries no sperm of mine. It was perhaps cruel to let her think it did and that with it she could conceive, at her pleasure, a royal prince.

If it was cruel of me, it was crueler to let the deception continue. But it was a way of speeding NoNo's departure from Farland—with what she

thought to be a token portion of my actual self. I had not summoned her, you must know, and her presence here had begun to cloy.

But you must know that your people and mine are incompatible genetically. The club members must have told you that I am not humanoid but can appear that way if I wish it. Had I appeared in my own shape there could have been no companionship with NoNo, because there are no points of contact. Would she have been smitten if she had seen me the way Skwp once clinically described me, as "a malappendaged monstrosity, often unstable"? No, no.

I give no empty gifts. There is something of value in the capsule NoNo wears but nothing of mine. It is a human seed, Jack. It is yours.

You see, when I was considering a suitable farewell gift to NoNo and decided on the locket, I knew its contents would have to be special and appropriate. Because she and I were incompatible, in more ways than one, I dispatched a trusted emissary to the Northside sperm emporium you are sometimes forced by nature of your business, and by your own nature, to patronize. Your specimen was resold to my trusted messenger and packaged for star travel to Farland.

Was this merely a royal jest? I think not. It was my way of ensuring that NoNo would have a human child if she wanted one in this way, and not a space monster. The decision, with the happy news I've had of your impending marriage, is now yours, my friend.

Whether you value its contents, the locket itself is valuable. Tiffany's would give you a breathtaking estimate. Consider that if you are tempted to destroy it.

I have news of my own. My first true and sanctioned royal son is soon to be born. He will take my former name, Leo, and when he suc-

ceeds to the throne he will be Leo IX. Not a jest, but amusing, is it not?

An affectionate farewell from afar.

Potent VIII

Having read the astonishing document I yelled at the group at the bar: "Who the hell said I was going to marry NoNo?"

The reply was a combination of alien shrugs.

"Damn it," I said, waving Leo's letter, "what have you been up to?"

"Have a drink on the house," Boots said. "Sit down and talk about it, whatever it is."

"Don't pretend you haven't read every word of it." I accepted the beer. "I want to know what else you've been up to."

"Good news about Leo Reo's boy," JorenzO said. "Kings should have male heirs." He raised a glass. "Here's to everybody's happiness."

"Not a word about any of this to NoNo," I said.

"Word of honor," Boots said. "Whatever she is to know must come from you."

"And what is she to know, you conspirators?"

"What you tell her," he said. "No conspiracy here."

"A pseudolensing eavesdropper, a black magician, a scribe who knows everybody's secrets—and you tell me nothing is going on?"

"It's your move, actually," Boots said.

"What do you mean? Do you see something?"

Diskie appeared out of nowhere. "NoNo is coming," he said. "Oh, hello, Jack. Congratulations."

"Now listen—"

"Inside NoNo McCanless today is tranquility." Diskie spun sideways and disappeared, then came back in sight. "Inside Jack Norkus, on the other hand— You're all riled up, aren't you?"

"Just stay the hell out of me," I yelled. "And out of NoNo too."

"I think he's beginning to move," Boots said.

NoNo came in then. There was a spring in her step

and she smiled when she saw us. "Hello, boys. Hello, Jack."

"Hello, N— Hello. I've got to talk to you."

"Call me NoNo. I don't mind. Come to my booth."

"And give these galoots an earful?"

"Oh, that kind of talk. They're going to know anyhow, sooner or later, so it might as well be sooner."

"Know what?" I asked. Was she doing it too?

"Whatever there is to know. What anybody says anywhere." She was smiling again. She looked good, head high.

"What the hell," I said. "We'll take the booth. Want a drink?"

"A little white wine over ice."

I purposely dropped my voice. "And I'll have another beer."

Boots had them at the table almost before we sat down.

"Surbis?" Boots said. I sensed that under his furry face he was all smiles. "If you want anything else just think—I mean *ring*." He went back to the bar.

"Why so merry, my lady?" I asked.

"Compared to my previous morbid state? The book goes well, for one thing."

"What book?"

"What book? Nina Queen's book. Everybody knows what book. Don't pretend."

"Writing it out of your system?"

"It or him. But it's more than just that. Another him is in it too."

"Your father."

"Yes, and other hims. I think of you sometimes when I write and you do creep in now and again. Then there's the capital-H Him that father preached about, Christ's extraterrestrial brother."

"You could call it 'The Hymn of Him'."

She laughed. "That would be better than my working title."

"Is it fiction or nonfiction?"

"A little of both, I suppose."

"May I read it?"

"It's still rough. Could we have another drink?"

Boots was there instantly, serving us. "Actually, it reads very well," he said. "Surbis."

"Damn you, Boots," I said. "Get out of here."

"Thank you, Boots," NoNo said. "But tell Jack I didn't give it to you to read."

Boots nodded and went away.

"He was grinning, wasn't he?" I asked.

She agreed. "Twinkling, I'd say."

"All right. We know there's no privacy. What's this about a wedding? You're aware of the talk?"

"I have been for some days. I think it's rather amusing. And sweet."

"I just heard about it. I've been away, thinking."

"I've thought a lot lately, too."

"That's what we've got to talk about," I said. "Everybody knows what you and I are thinking except you and me. How did you hear about the wedding? Who told you?"

"Nobody told me. It just came into my mind one evening as I sat here and I knew it must have come from one of them. I'd had no thoughts like it before, at least not since we were kids reading Father's books together, and that childish thought was mixed up with others about finding my Prince Charming on Mars or Venus."

"Is it still a childish thought? What was your reaction aside from its being amusing and sweet?"

"That was my reaction to them for putting it in my mind. About such a wedding—I don't reject the idea utterly. On the other hand, I haven't sent announcements to our near and dear."

She was no longer smiling and I realized I had been grilling her about an intimate matter without giving her an indication of my feelings. "Surbis," I said. "I'll admit I've thought about marriage more recently than that time in your father's study. Marrying you. We are talking about you and me, aren't we?"

"Yes. That is the hypothetical subject. Did you think about that before or after I went—chased off after Leo?"

"Before," I said. "Only before, until today."

She put her hand on the table, close to but not touching her glass, and I took it. It was a gentle clasp and we looked at each other without speaking. After a little while we were grinning and broke into laughter.

"You tell me," she said.

"I was thinking that my thoughts were so mixed up that I'd have to ask the eavesdroppers what was really in my mind."

"Me too."

Boots was there again before I said, "I'm starved," and before I realized he hadn't brought another round of drinks but was setting sandwiches before us.

"So that's what you were thinking!" NoNo said, laughing.

"I assure you that was the least of his thoughts, my dear," Boots told her.

As we ate we talked about inconsequential things.

Then I said: "Now we have to talk about the locket."

"I was afraid of that," NoNo said.

§ § §

After the sweetness of that scene I declined to detail the agony of our talk about the locket. Boots and his buddies heard it all, and Scoop can retrieve it for you if your interest is more scholarly than prurient—or even if it isn't.

I told NoNo I'd had a letter from Leo. That surprised her, and she asked to see it. I said he had written in confidence and I would respect that trust. She spoke angrily about trust for a man who had betrayed her. I said he was not a man. She said she knew him better than I and that he was a man. I said she had been deceived, opthalmologically, linguapathophonically and in other ways. I explained. She wept. She said that if that was so he'd been kind not to let her see him as he really was. I agreed it was a kind of kindness. I said it had been gracious of him to tell no one that he had not sent for her, that she had bought her own ticket to Farland. More tears.

Because he was not a man, I told her, she could not have his child. The species were incompatible, I said, ignoring the other incompatibility of which he'd spoken. All things were possible, she said. He would not have given her the locket if— Exobiologists disagreed, I said. I'd plumbed Scoop to his depths on the subject. Besides—

She blew her nose and wanted to know besides what. I hesitated, but she seemed to have recovered her composure, and after a long pause I told her it was not his seed in the locket. Not his, but— I had to blurt it out: not his but mine.

All the antagonism was wiped from her face as she tried to understand, to accept. Her voice was dull, her face blank as she asked how that could be. Ashamed, I told her. Her face clouded.

It wasn't true, she said at last. Leo had heard the rumors of a wedding—rumors planted, no doubt, by our well-meaning but meddling otherworldly friends—and was lying to be kind. She didn't believe my exobiologists. Whatever it might cost us, she would have his child.

But I could not let her have that child, knowing it mine, if she believed it his. Not if we were to marry.

We needn't marry for her to have the child, she pointed out. These weren't the old days.

They were the old days for her father and mother, the grandparents, I pointed out. Had she thought of them?

Often, she said. She thought her father would accept the child, whatever its form, and baptize it in vindication of his belief, and that her mother would go along, as she always had.

But what about me, I asked, hurting. If it turned out, and I believed this, that it was my seed, was I to be denied fatherhood?

She said I'd denied it when I went to that filthy place and sold a piece of myself. Leo had bought and paid for it but that didn't prove it was in the locket.

I said she had sent me there in frustration because of the way she had carried on with me among a dozen males, most of them aliens, during the wildest of her wild ways, in whatever frenzy was upon her then.

She wept again, saying that was long ago and she had hoped we were different now, able to accept the once unacceptable, to be friends and live with the realities of today and of the future.

I was weeping with her and said I'd like us to have a new start. Let's the two of us go off to a cleaner, greener land and sink the locket in the lake I'd found and go on from there together.

With a conventional wedding night and everything, she said. Was that what I wanted?

I said yes it was. Sink the damned locked and go to bed on our honeymoon with nothing between her breasts but her own sweet skin. Without a seed that had been exposed to God knows what influences on two journeys through space.

You're asking for everything or nothing, Jack, aren't you? Take it off, sink it, forget all it may mean and the hell with my feelings.

Yes, I am. For both of us.

No, Jack. There are three of us now. Never, Jack. No, No.

§ § §

I must have been deranged after that talk with NoNo to seek out JorenzO the Black Magician. But he'd often been kind to us. Furthermore she'd never flung herself into his lap, probably because his awesome dignity would not have permitted it.

"I know you're not a seer," I told JorenzO, "but your other magical powers might help me."

JorenzO smiled down at me from his seven feet of metal body and costume. He was black as an old kettle except in the stiff steel fiber of his iron-gray hair.

"You are here at the right time. I have just purchased the mechanicals of an act of Spanish seers, a trio accredited by the Futurology Society. For half a century, your time, they were prognosticators without peer. Even you must know of them. They billed themselves as Prog, Nost, & Kate; or, in Hispanic, Prog, Nost, y Kate. I have bought their book for a sum that will permit them to live out their lives in comfort in Barcelona. I had to be generous, for they know how long that will be."

"Fine," I said. "I congratulate you. Can you help me? I have no money."

Always magical, he was now oracular. Lofty but friendly, he said he would find a solution by probing the future. He was between tours and would do this for me in friendship.

He told me how it would be. I'd be flung into an alternate future, one of several I told him I'd considered. In that future I'd rejected NoNo after she had rejected me and had her child from the locket.

"Expect nightmare," he said. "Expect the unexpected you have asked for. I will show you a future you may not like, though it is there."

I told him I needed to know, however repugnant it might be.

"Then tomorrow night we travel," JorenzO said. "You will see it plain and then must choose whether it is to be or whether there is another way."

Boots took me aside and said, surprising me by his criticism of a fellow alien: "Don't rely too much on JorenzO. It will be chancy, especially to someone like you who can't know the effect it will have on you. Consider that its complexities may have been too much for those of us who have traveled part of that path, then retreated to find a haven here in a backwater of the cosmos—forgive me, Earthman—where things are easier and, if there's little excitement, there's a kind of peace. Talk to NoNo again. Don't fling yourself so far that you can't get back."

But we had talked, NoNo and I. God how we'd talked. In the club, downside at her place, my place, at cafeterias and bars, in parks.

Both of us wanted peace, comfort, ease, and laughter whether together or apart. We were honest about that. We'd prefer together, having known each other a long time, although in scattered segments. Was there another for her or me? For her, no, unless she still believed in a far prince. For me, only my neater, sweeter maiden, who might well be she—not another person but herself returned and different (why did I think repentant?) and was I vengeful, demanding that she renounce her dreams yet again? I may have been; I too have my wild side. Inside myself (Diskie knows) I've been as frantic as she; but I stored it up, not giving it out except those times at the sperm bank when I'd succumbed, as she never had. Could she be my almost virginal bride?

We came to no conclusion after again exploring the possibilities. One: She could have the child of the locket, hoping and believing it Leo's. Or she could agree that it was mine and decline it, preferring the real me, not a surrogate but my flesh in hers. (Fat chance, from all she'd said.) There was still unbridgable distance between us, despite all the conversation.

We reached the hour JorenzO had set for my journey in space and time. He must have known there'd be no resolution and that his experiment would be the alternative.

We were in a small auditorium. Its edges were dark; I could see no walls. The stage was dim with shapes that had no meaning. Boots had seated NoNo and me a good distance apart on a curving riser. He sat between us, next to her.

JorenzO appeared on the stage in a cloud of black smoke. Diskie entered, glimmering almost subliminally, then winked out. Scoop came and occupied an aisle, needing no seat, all attuned, all business.

JorenzO said: "We are assembled to help our

friends. Let the record show this."

Diskie reappeared from inside JorenzO. "The record will show what it will show. Action now, words later. Like Lopi making a film."

"First prologue," JorenzO said, recapitulating as if for archives. "NoNo has declined to destroy the locket. She is no longer positive it encloses the seed of the Far King but still believes there is a chance to bear a royal child. If she believed the seed to be Jack's, destroying it would be a betrayal of Jack, of whom she is fond. She is also residually fond of the Far King. Both men have been cads, but all men are cads, she reasons. Jack will not have her while she wears the locket. Impasse. Let the drama begin." He left the stage to sit near me.

A disembodied voice spoke from among the dim shapes before us: "The time is future, and what you will see is reality. NoNo, estranged from Jack, had the child of the locket. The child was male and human, as she expected it to be, whoever the father. She called him Star Kin. Kin, not quite King. Kin grew and developed normally. NoNo, who thought of herself as Ann Bagley, was happy. She invited Jack to visit, to see the child. He visited once, knew the boy to be his, was convinced the child was his, certain of it but unwilling to forget that NoNo had chosen to risk the possibility of it being Leo Reo's. Jack was unwilling to be friends with her. She half hoped there might be a reconciliation but it seemed impossible." The voice went on and the shapes began to assume scenes from the narrative:

Jack brooded, refused to visit again.

NoNo left Chicago with Kin and returned to her father's house. She was the prodigal daughter, welcomed, accepted by grandparents proud of their Kin. She was content, a good mother, and read again in her father's books and worked on her own.

Kin continued to grow, but no longer normally. His development accelerated. Eight months after birth he had the body and mind of a boy of six years. Kin's grandparents marveled. A miracle! Kin talked but said little. He read much, mostly in his grandfather's books and in his mother's manuscript.

NoNo marveled at her son. Not a miracle to her, but evidence that Leo had lied, or Jack had lied, and that she had indeed borne the child of a Far King, lord of a realm where time is different.

The minister's village and flock were not yet ready either for a miracle or a starbegotten child; and Kin was kept in the house, as if he were still an infant.

Word of the phenomenal growth reached Jack, who believed neither in a miracle nor that the child was Leo's. He was convinced that Kin was his, born of a seed that had traveled twice across the cosmos, first with Leo's emissary, then back in NoNo's locket, subjected to unknowable extrasolar emissions and influences.

Jack's brooding intensified. He was granted live-in privileges at the 5280 Club and abandoned his business to spend hours poring over theological works Scoop produced from alien archives as well as from his growing terrestrial collection. As a boy in Ezekiel Bagley's study, Jack never thought he'd accept literally any of the clergyman's hand-me-down ideas. Who could have foreseen that the catalyst to his conversion would be the fruit of his own loins, implanted antiseptically in the womb of Ann-Bagley-become-NoNo-McCanless? Anyone who lived among the aliens in the 5280 Club eventually became a little crazy, but Jack took pride in the fact that his research didn't persuade him that he was Jesus Christ. Too many had done that bit. No, sir, he was father to the Jesus of the worlds afar. His son Kin was the Other Christ. Kin, son of God, brother to Jesus, son of God, and immaculately conceived.

Having heard that Kin—one year old in Earth time—looked, acted, and *was* 12 years old, Jack heard another Word and kidnapped his son.

Kin went willingly with his father to the Mile-Hi Building, as if he'd been waiting for his ministry to begin. At the 5280 Club Jack asked JorenzO the Black Magician to seek a place beyond the world that already had a Christ. JorenzO said there'd be no fee; he'd take a profit some way.

JorenzO said: "Board the Midnight Shipment and transfer at The Wait. Ask for Darkohl; everybody will understand. Think Dark Hole. It's a bar not unlike this one. Give Captain Black Otro this card. He'll book you and the boy on the shuttle to Dyson. It's the only way and the only place. Do you know what you're doing? Only you can judge."

Jack said he was sure and took the card. Boots was in the background, saying nothing but seeming to lean toward disapproval.

Kin and Jack reached The Wait and found the shuttle. They were assigned places below and awoke for the glide down to Dyson. Maybe Kin was growing faster now or maybe his sleep below in star time contributed, but when he set foot on the planet he looked a tall, strapping, bearded twenty-one.

It was a good place for them to start, in this craggy desert land whose people could have been their Earth brothers of Biblical times but who had never heard the Word.

For now Kin carried out his first ministry and he and his father (and, presumably, his Father) were content.

But one morning Kin went to his human father and said, "I have had a vision." Jack was pleased until Kin continued. "Mother tried to die because of what we have done."

Jack was troubled. "I am sorry to hear that. But what is done and will be done is the Lord's work."

"I understand but I am saddened. Grandfather found her in time and with God's help she will be restored to health."

"Praise the Lord," Jack said.

"But she is distraught and disturbed. She spends her time sculpting little statues. There are so many that the church is selling them to help its building fund."

"When did it happen, this that you saw in the vision?"

"It seemed that it was a time ago." They spoke no more of it. Later they stood on a mountaintop, leaning on their staffs, content with their work in the valley behind them. Ahead lay another place that needed the Word. And, when they had gone down and enlightened them, there would be other places, other worlds eager to receive them. So spoke Jack to his son, the Son of God, for was it not written that there were many worlds to which God's Majesty reached? That it was not only the bipeds of Earth that He watched over but also the creatures of lands beyond who were as dear to Him, in their various shapes, as were they.

They went down the rocky path and came to a marketplace. A stall displayed figures of bestial shape. Heathen idols, Jack thought, and raised his staff to smash them. But Kin grasped his wrist and bade him look more closely. Could it be a miracle? Was it a sign of the Lord's interstellar omniscience? On that distant planet was evidence that Another had preceded them.

The old woman who tended the stall proffered first one, then another of the clay figures. They were exquisitely made, representing creatures of a dozen worlds whose like he had seen before—Boots and JorenzO and Diskie and Lopi and Mogle and Scoop. Memories of the alien-touched Earth he had renounced! Memories of NoNo—who else could have sculpted them?

But he ignored the old woman's offerings because on a shelf back of her were larger, choicer pieces so true to life that his limbs began to tremble. One was of Leo Reo in a robe that made him look like a Judas. The other was of his son Kin, with a halo over his head. Jack purchased the second, thinking it strange that the halo was attached at the front. When they reached the inn to which they were traveling they saw that the halo had broken off, leaving a scar where it had been fastened to the forehead.

In a dream at the inn that night Jack was troubled by a thought that his son was not his but Adam's and that Kin would slay not his brother, because he had none, but his father.

Had NoNo cursed him across the cosmos? He awoke in sweat, trembling to hear his son suggest that they leave the marked path for a way through the cane fields. He was sore afraid to go but in the end he went, as he knew he must.

Kin's smiling lips and his mother's eyes beckoned him and he followed his son into the barren landscapes where the dead husks rustled in the hot breeze and the alien sun was a blood-red disc behind a haze.

Kin was arrested, charged with and found guilty of patricide and executed at the scene of the crime as the new crop came up in the cane fields. Method of execution: crucifixion, head down. A multitude of people on the primitive planet watched. Contrary to folk tales, there was no resurrection. Kin's body was taken down and incinerated. His ashes fertilized the field.

§ § §

The multitudes of the primitive, Earthlike planet vanished as the house lights came on full. "What the hell goes on here?" Lopi yelled. "Who said you could use my set?"

I shuddered and felt nauseated as I was yanked back from the future drama where I'd been both spectator and participant. I blinked in the glare and looked past the audience of aliens to NoNo. She was touching her locket in a questioning way and seemed relieved to see me alive.

"It was a JorenzO production in a good cause," Boots said mildly. "An attempt to solve the problems of two friends."

"When I need a co-producer it won't be JorenzO,"

Lopi said. "You damn amateurs! Did you damage any of my props?"

"Only a halo on a little statue," NoNo said. "I'll make you another. And we almost lost Jack."

"We did lose him," JorenzO said, giving Lopi a black look. "We saw—lived—the future. It happened in the part of time that is a projection of now. What has happened is past and therefore true."

"It was a projection all right," Lopi stormed. "My stage manager says you ran a tape of my epic in progress, 'The Death of God in Dyson.' It should make a mint wherever they eat missionaries." He turned to JorenzO. "And you thought you could pass it off as one of your feats of magic? I should sue you for plagiarism, you fake necromancer."

"It happened," JorenzO said with dignity. "All of us saw. Fortunately the future is reversible."

"Sure," Lopi said. "You rewind the tape."

"Excellently put," Boots said. "Have you considered, Lopi, that All-Planets Films could be liable for invading the privacy of two of our guests?"

Lopi was adaptable. He said: "Okay, I won't show it in the solar area. You drop invasion of privacy, I drop plagiarism. Now will you get the hell out of my screening room and let me work? NoNo, dear, the halo statue; this time make the scar a little more visible, okay? Surbis, Jack, for killing you off, but it's only a picture, for Christ's sake. Did you like your son?"

"Up to a point," I said, feeling better. "Cane fields aren't my thing."

"I adored him," NoNo said. "I'm going to have him."

§ § §

Lopi stayed and the rest of us went to the club for restoratives, Boots buying. It was good to be back in the familiar now, the future nightmare dimming as the tape rewound.

NoNo and I sat in her far booth and the others grouped around. There was camaraderie. Accommodation seemed possible. Boots served NoNo a glittering luminescent wine and gave me a beer with bubbles golden and tangy.

There we were, Norkus, Bagley & Co. It sounded like the pair of professional mountebanks we were in JorenzO's purloined scenario, flinging ourselves across the cosmos in an orgy of revenge, blaming our derangement not on our faulty selves but on the Rev. Ezekiel Bagley's charming and terrible interpretation of the Bible. Scoop said the old boy might be right about there being some higher plan in the diversity of worlds but that it probably would take an intercosmic ecumenical congress to work it out.

Having lived vicarious years during the screening—for NoNo and me it was decades—we had come back to ourselves changed. Earlier the different time of Farland had subtly aged NoNo. Now I felt tired to my bones. Had part of myself gone on that future journey? Had it happened? JorenzO said it had, even if reversibly. Everything that could happen on one path or another had happened and it had depleted me.

Now I saw that NoNo had aged once more. It was physical, a bit, in the way she carried herself, the way she spoke. But deeper than that was a new look of maturity and wisdom.

I suppose I was different and wiser too. Thoughts relayed by the aliens flew between us. We had been drifters. We had been barren, not just of children who could be our only immortality, but of purpose. An aimless future lay ahead, unless—

Neither of us wanted to experience another possible future unless it was one we controlled, having just been through a thoroughly nasty one. Theatrical and semi-fictional as it was, it had been a catharsis.

NoNo and I exchanged glances and little smiles as the alien telepathy worked to catalyze and exchange our thoughts. Of course they'd had it in mind, those clever conspirators, to jolt us in this way or another into reconsidering our once inflexible positions.

Now NoNo and I were touching hands and talking, oblivious to the alien eavesdroppers we knew would always be with us, all friends, all honorary godfathers.

When No No voiced the solution, which seemed to have sprung simultaneously from the massed minds of a dozen planets, it received unanimous approval. Boots was particularly happy. He was the last of his kind.

NoNo spoke for all of us:

"My friends, listen. Only recently I still believed, or hoped, that I would be the queen of a far king, if not the Far King I'd known. I was proud and arrogant but I've been humbled by the concern that my friends, old and new, have shown for me. Now I think the coming king is not one I'll marry but one I'll mother. As JorenzO has shown me, he is Kin, but as all of you have assured me, he will live a different life than that of Lopi's scenario.

"And Kin will have a twin, conceived in a private old-fashioned way, but who, with the help of our new-fashioned eugenics, will be a girl. In her lifetime she will have the opportunity to be the queen of a far land, but probably she'll be just as happy to be the consort of a man here on Earth—a prince of a fellow, if not of alien seed.

"Will anyone know which of the twins was star-begotten and which the product of a conventional conception? Possibly you will know but I think it better that you never tell the parents."

It was lump in the throat time as Boots refilled our glasses and we toasted each other.

Then Scoop became animated and produced a scroll from one of the outputs of himself and said: "Hear! A message from the Far King, once Leo Reo, now Potent VIII of Farland, as follows: 'The next Midnight Shipment will bring as my nuptial gift to the happy couple two royal lockets for their twins, should they aspire, in a score of years, to leave Earth in a vicarious way by seeking far mates. For now, give them a fond kiss from their stepfather."

NoNo and I locked eyes and I told Scoop to send Leo a message: "I appreciate the thought but on receipt of the lockets, whatever their intrinsic value or contents, we'll take them to another state and sink them in a lake I know. Sign it John Northcrosse, formerly nobody, now mate-to-be of the former NoNo McCanless, now a new person."

NoNo, the dear Ann of our youth, said: "Tell Leo I agree absolutely. And tell him to go jump in the lake."

Dan McQuarrie assured us there was a linguapathic equivalent for the idiom that Leo would understand.

Now, in a special alien suite a mile above Earth with a window overlooking the Midnight Shipment, NoNo and I, content, await the birth of our terrestrial twins.

A THIRD SOLUTION TO THE THIRD DR. MOREAU
(from page 153)

If the process starts with two microbes, then after each hour the number will be double the corresponding number in the sequence that starts with one microbe. After 48 hours, twice the number of microbes is not enough to make the container 1/7 full, so the correct answer is 49 hours. At that time the container becomes 2/7 full.